The PERFECT PULL

a novel by

Lindsay Woolman

Playa Blanca
MEDIA

For my mom,
who has always believed in me

If you could only know
All that I see
All that I feel
All that I hear
In your hair
Your hair contains a dream in its entirety,
filled with sails and masts.

~Charles Baudelaire

chapter one

You could say I know a lot about hair, but that would be an understatement. I know how each tiny follicle makes an imprint on my skin and I know that I am fascinated by the texture of hair between my fingertips. I know that it takes a few days to a month for one hair to grow back. I have known this since I was in the fourth grade and locked into the bathroom with my best friend.

We are filling up the sink with warm water. A pink razor blade sits on the counter like a dead insect in a museum. I imagine the blade against my skin and don't want to go there, but my mother's words ring in my ears: "Alyssa, your legs look like a monkey's butt."

"Let's do this," I say to Kat.

"Right on," she says.

I run my hands over the hairs one last time before we lather my legs with shaving cream. I can almost imagine whole planets and worlds taking place between the pores where the hairs grew out, only they would be giant buildings with tiny, gnarly people living inside. I have a huge imagination, which is part of the reason I am afraid to shave my legs. I picture something terrible will happen, like I might break into a bleeding fit and end up in the ER next to a guy who choked on a potato chip.

"We still need shaving cream," Kat says, filling the sink with warm water.

"It's in here somewhere," I say, sifting through shampoo bottles in the cupboard where my mom keeps a stockpile. I hold out a sample size bottle and grin as if posing for an infomercial. "Found it."

"I'll take that," Kat says, shaking it up and spraying some into the palm of her hand.

Kat is the most popular girl in our class and my best friend. People like to make comments that we are like sisters because we can finish each other's sentences, but that's where the similarities end. While Kat is blessed with emerald eyes and blonde hair that cascades down her back like a waterfall, my hair is thin and reddish brown like a tree trunk with curls that wrap around my shoulders. Plus, my eyes change from blue to gray as if they aren't sure of their color.

Together, we spread the shaving cream over my calves and up to my knees and Kat splashes the razor in the sink, making a mess. I watch with satisfaction as water spills over the marble countertop and onto the floor.

My mother, Vivian, is a clean freak and would probably faint if she saw the mess we are making right now.

Kat takes the razor and I shut my eyes tightly. I can't watch. The idea of something sharp against my skin scares me. I feel her drawing it gently up my leg and open my eyes, realizing nothing bad is happening. It's all so easy I can hardly believe it.

After we finish both legs, I unplug the drain. I watch the hairs littering the sides of the sink and feel a shiver.

Kat has found one of Vivian's lipsticks and applies it carefully on her lips. Then she kisses the mirror and admires her fuchsia colored lips, smacking them together.

"Uh, we probably shouldn't play with my mom's makeup stuff on the mirror," I say, rubbing coconut scented lotion over my silky legs. I can't imagine the kind of trouble I'll be in if Vivian finds out we're going through her things.

"We'll clean it up," Kat chimes in, pressing her lips to the mirror again. "She only has like a million lipsticks in the drawer, not to mention every cleaning product in the world."

"True," I agree, still feeling nervous.

Kat pulls a few more things out of the drawer, including a magnified mirror. It is brave of us to go through my mother's makeup and private stuff, as I've never done anything like this before.

I hold up the magnified mirror, checking out my face and chin and neck. Sure enough, one single hair I noticed a few weeks ago is still under my chin. Maybe we could shave it off next. I suggest the idea to Kat.

"You can't shave your face, Alyssa. You'll end up looking like the Weasel."

"That's a scary thought."

"Yeah, so don't even think about it."

The Weasel is a boy in our fourth grade class who has already developed peach fuzz above his upper lip. Kat thinks he matured early because of eating too many chicken nuggets that were not organic. I just feel bad for the kid.

Whenever I look at the Weasel and his peach fuzz, it is

9

something I don't want to notice, but then once my eyes lock in, it is hard to stop staring. It is kind of like seeing pictures of naked people or people who've had operations or lesions on their bodies. You know you shouldn't look too carefully, but you can't help yourself.

"What am I supposed to do with it, then?" I ask.

"Use tweezers," Kat insists. "I'm sure the Barbie Lady has a pair around here."

"That's a good idea," I say, hearing my mother's nickname float into the air.

My mother's real name is Vivian Marissa Simone, but she has had enough plastic surgery to earn herself the famous nickname and Internet superstar status. She has a website where she details her surgery expeditions like they are travel stories. She regularly makes an appearance on an L.A. morning show, and her before and after photos are plastered all over the Internet.

I keep very quiet about her craziness to my classmates and friends, but Vivian is hard to miss. She has icicle blue eyes, enhanced lips, stunning blonde hair, and a body that turns heads.

Vivian is a rep for Glamour Prix Cosmetics, a company started by my father Milton. They have bragging rights to a line of lipsticks that claims to plump your lips over time and she makes videos about her many procedures and gives cosmetic surgery advice to the curious. Vivian and my father own other businesses together too. One of them, Event-Edge, hosts parties for companies around the world. I don't know why my parents want to constantly travel since we live in a big house near the ocean in San Diego, but that's just what they do.

My father likes to spend time either in his office or on an

airplane. When Vivian isn't busy chatting with her adoring fans or cleaning the house, she is planning outings and driving around in her Lexus. It's not that bad, and I shouldn't complain, but sometimes when I'm alone at night I feel like I don't have a real family.

"Where are your parents tonight?" Kat asks.

"They're in Orange County until late."

"So I guess you'll be sleeping over at my house?"

"Is that okay?" I ask. "My suitcase is ready to go."

"Of course. My family loves you."

"Let's pluck that hair out before we go," she suggests.

"Okay," I say, with a bit too much enthusiasm.

I take the pair of tweezers, feeling the metal and black rubber grip. If only the sky could have opened at that moment and snatched them away from me.

I lean in close to the mirror and bravely pluck it out—a sharp, bright pinch. Instead of letting the hair go, I place it on my thumb and rub it between my fingertips, noticing a tiny, white bulb at the end, like a pearl.

"Make a wish and blow it off your finger," Kat says. "That's what you're supposed to do with hairs."

Strangely, I don't want to let it go.

"Here, I'll do it with you," she says, rubbing her eye until she had a stray eyelash. She places it on her thumb, showing me. "Ready?"

We take a breath and blow it out together.

I wish Josh Slater would kiss me, I think silently.

Let me tell you about Josh. He is this kid in our class who is cute and clumsy and kind of a nerd. He has dirty blonde hair that falls into his eyes and he wears glasses and he's always bumping into walls because that's just the way he is. He also has a way of opening his mouth a little too wide while talking or chewing gum, and I can't help but notice his lips.

They can suck an entire soda down without him using his hands. I think about kissing him and wonder what else he could do with his lips. I know I shouldn't be thinking this stuff, but it just comes to me sometimes.

I don't tell Kat how I feel about Josh, liking the idea of kissing him as my secret. Kat and I have a pact that we're supposed to tell each other *everything*, but there are limits, you know? Kissing Josh is one of those things for me.

Another secret I keep is about my imaginary friend. I invented her a few years ago to keep me company at night when my parents weren't home. Her name is Aurora Stone and even though she doesn't actually exist, I imagine she lives in the countryside and goes to school just like everyone else. I know I'm too old for imaginary friends, but Aurora is different.

I picture her living in a world that is exactly like this one, except more exciting. I pretend that Aurora has a boyfriend named Hoffman Black who lives next door to her, and only I can see into their lives. Aurora is blessed with long, wavy blonde hair that goes all the way to her waist like a mermaid, and sometimes I draw pictures of her in my notebooks instead of doing my homework. Only I can see into her life, watching all the dramas that unfold.

Aurora helps pass the time when I am alone, which is often. She is beautiful and capable and everything I want to be. She never messes up anything or acts weak or weird. I make her popular, like Kat, except she is nicer. She never takes anything without asking and she is nice without needing anything in return.

I wish the world were really like that, that people were always nice and that no one could hurt anyone.

Kat has a bossy streak and these unpredictable mood swings. I wouldn't want another best friend, but sometimes she bugs me.

"Check out your elbow," Kat says, grabbing my arm and twisting it around. "There are a lot of hairs growing out of that thing."

I twist my arm slightly more to discover the mole with the mysterious hairs curling out of it like daddy long legs. It amazes me that I have never seen them before and they've been growing on my body all this time.

"Where did those tweezers go?" she asks, eyeing the bathroom counter.

"Let's just leave it," I say. "I'm tired of playing beauty parlor."

I don't want to admit it, but I am very curious about the hairs and can't wait to be alone to examine them. I can already hear the questions in my mind:

Why are they so black they are almost blue?

Why do they grow out of the mole like that?

Why are they disgusting and interesting to me?

That night at Kat's house when I am in the bathroom, I bravely pluck each hair from the mole, one by one, watching carefully as my skin stretches just as the hair pops out. The pain is so severe that it makes my eyes water, but I want to do it again.

I have to pull those hairs in the same way I have to straighten up my socks if they are turned the wrong way in my shoes. It is like an itch I have to scratch. It is a ripple in the water I have to reach out and dip my fingers into.

I can't help myself.

chapter two

BANG, BANG!

"Just a minute," I say, as Vivian's fist pounds on the bathroom door.

I shove the tweezers into my makeup bag, hiding them like they are a pack of cigarettes. I've never tried a cigarette, but Vivian might approve of them more than what I am doing right now.

"Be right out," I say, trying to convey in my voice I am doing something important, like flossing. Then I glance in the mirror and focus on my pupils like I am seeing them for the first time.

My eyes are gray and vacant. They always look this way after I spend too much time in the bathroom. I shake some loose brown curls from my hair into my face, wishing I'd never come in here. I turned fifteen this summer and my hair is lighter, with red highlights from a summer of beach days spent with Kat and our group of friends. It has taken me forever to grow out my hair so that when I take a curl and straighten it, it reaches my bra strap.

When I open the door, Vivian is in one of her signature Barbie Lady outfits, which consists of a fitted purple t-shirt dress with glitter writing that says "goddess," high heeled sandals, and gobs of bracelets. Her long wavy hair is combed over one shoulder.

"What are your plans today?" she asks, her blue eyes so intensely focused on mine that I can't blink. "You know you have high school orientation, right?"

I sigh. "I remember."

I've already completed my freshman year and now I am at the bottom of the barrel again. I am about to begin at an unfamiliar school that starts with sophomore year. I don't know anyone at this school, or in this city, and I don't want to be here.

It was Vivian's idea for us to move.

Two weeks ago, we filled the backseat and trunk of her newest silver Lexus with suitcases of clothes and accessories. The car is like her second child, a gift from my dad, Milton. She loves the car so much that she never drives in the rain just to keep it nice and shiny.

Good thing it doesn't rain much in Las Vegas because that's where we are heading, and there is no garage to put it in now. We are the newest occupants of an unremarkable yellow house so very unlike our picturesque home near the cliffs in San Diego. The house belonged to my grandmother and I think she has owned it since when the dinosaurs roamed here.

Grandma Mackey passed away in April and Vivian had this crazy idea that we should live inside the house and apply to be on the home makeover show, *Kicking it at Grandma's House.* I never thought it would happen, but then the show picked us to be the newest reality show stars.

The Home and Garden Channel is filming the house transformation until December, when Vivian promises the house will get sold off to the highest bidder, and we will return to our regularly scheduled lives in California.

The way she explains it, our stint in Vegas is a package deal, a chance to do something good and get TV time in the process. I guess it also depends on how you define "good."

"Alyssa, you should be excited. People around the world are going to recognize you from the show. We're going to be a household name," she told me.

I know I *should* be excited about the prospect of strangers recognizing me on the street, but I'm not. The whole thing makes me nervous. What if I say something stupid? What if I look horrible on camera or have boogers coming out of my nose and start talking and burp instead? What if the truth comes out that I have a zit colony on my chin and have never been kissed?

Plus, there's a giant problem with my family. We're crumbling like a sand castle in an earthquake.

I pretend I know nothing, as usual. But I found the notes from my father's girlfriend with her pretty cursive handwriting and heart-shaped dots over the "i" in his name. I don't know why she couldn't have just texted or emailed him, but maybe she likes to play it old school.

His girlfriend is a flight attendant and they are madly in love, and it makes sense because my father is a first class man. He'd fly through freeway traffic if he could. It's never fast enough.

When I found the notes, I felt like a character in a movie, with dramatic music overhead, watching myself put them back into the bottom of the drawer and backing away like I'd never breathed in that space before.

My father mostly just passes through our house like a ghost, so this information is too personal for words. He always has his phone in his hand and his mind in another time zone.

So it shouldn't really surprise me when Vivian pulls into the fast lane on the freeway going toward Vegas and casually mentions she knows too.

"But we're not getting a divorce," she insists, weaving through traffic. "Divorces are so cliché."

"Uh huh?" I have no idea where she is going with this, but that's Vivian for you. She is full of a million surprises, mostly bad ones.

"I might just as well find myself a boyfriend too," she adds, like it's a grand idea. She reaches into her purse and lights a cigarette, something she only does when stressed out. "We're thinking about having an open relationship. You know what that is, right?"

"Like polygamists?"

"No, sweetie. Your dad has girlfriends and I have boyfriends, but we stay married. We're still equals."

"Is that what you want?"

"I don't have a choice," she says, rubbing a bit of lipstick off the edge of her lip. "But this is private stuff, so I don't want you dishing this to your friends or the show or anyone else. Promise me?"

"I won't tell anyone. I have your back."

"Not even Kat. I know she has been your best friend since kindergarten, but her mom rides the gossip train."

"I won't say a word. I don't tell Kat everything, you know?"

"Good. The show wants us to convey the strength of our family, even with the tragic loss of Grandma." Vivian exhales a puff of smoke.

"Of course." I inhale the smoke, kind of liking the smell.

But the truth is that we haven't visited Grandma Mackey in

17

years. And from what I observed the moment we stepped into her little yellow house, I doubt she would have wanted a home makeover.

Grandma Mackey *loved* her junk.

When I say loved, I mean her house is a museum. We're talking decaying animal skulls in the front yard, a collection of merry-go-round horses in the living room, a roof filled with miniature reindeer and a Jesus figure in a sled with a red knitted hat on his plastic head.

It looks like no one has touched the place in *years*.

The house itself is kind of sunken into the ground with two large homes on either side towering above.

"I'm really sorry you're going to miss the first few months of school back home," Vivian adds. "Maybe when we return in December, Josh Slater will ask you out."

I think of Josh and gaze out the window at the red rocks in the distance. I wonder what could happen between now and then.

A few weeks earlier I had a going away party at our house and I wondered how Josh and I would say goodbye.

For the first time, he and I were getting closer, sending each other silly texts and flirting over the summer. We had finally become genuine friends and I often caught Josh staring at me, although I never could tell the reason. I'm not exactly easy to find in a crowd because I am short, but Josh and I managed to lock eyes every time we were near each other. He still wears his glasses and sometimes I wonder if it's just the glare from the glass or maybe he really is checking me out.

For the party Vivian helped me decorate the back patio with

flaming tiki torches and we strung white twinkle lights in the orange trees and around the deck. A cool evening breeze blew in from the ocean, a few blocks away.

I didn't want a big send off and I wasn't sure who to invite, so instead we just invited everyone. As in everyone on *Vivian's* list.

She keeps up with the happenings at my school even better than I do, gossiping with the girls and trying to be the cool, hip mom, which is extremely annoying. In fact, I think that is the reason I started called her Vivian. My friends all look up to her and talk about her like she is one of us.

But she doesn't know much below the surface.

Like that over the summer things changed. Kat has always been the unspoken leader in our group, but ever since she made the cheerleading squad, she has these new friends. Not to mention her growing list of boyfriends and make out buddies.

Even at this party, I can tell things are not the same.

I stroll out to the giant back deck wearing a loose tank top, cotton skirt, high heeled flip flops, and a delicate gold necklace dangling to my chest. My hair is pulled into a curly ponytail and I wrap one of the curls around my finger, taking the ponytail over my shoulder.

"Cheers," Kat says, handing me a margarita and pushing her clear plastic cup toward mine. "Here's to sophomore year."

"To this year," I reply, noticing how much taller Kat is than me, even with my high-heeled flip-flops.

"Too bad you're leaving me for half the year," she says. "I still can't believe you're going to miss my cheerleading debut."

"It's only four months," I correct her. "And you're going to send me the video clips, right?

"I will definitely do that," Kat says, putting down her drink and adjusting a bra strap. She is wearing a sleeveless royal blue sundress and I don't know if it is because of becoming a cheerleader or what, but over the summer everything about Kat has become unattainably cool.

"I still wish you were on the squad," she says.

"Me too," I lie.

Actually, we are both lying because jumping up and down in a short skirt really isn't my thing—and we both know it.

"I always imagined us cheering together, going to practices and football games," she adds. "I know you don't like the attention, but I think cheerleading would be good for you. Plus, you would be killer good at the stunts and flips."

"Maybe next year?"

"That would be fun." Kat takes out her phone and sends a text to someone. She is distracted as usual.

I'll admit I was relieved last spring when my final swim meet was the same day as her tryouts. I couldn't imagine going gaga over a touchdown, but I played along when Kat started practicing, acting like it mattered to me. Swimming is my passion, but being underwater isn't as sexy.

Except I haven't set foot in the pool or ocean in months.

I am trying to ignore the strange problem I have. But when I am in the bathroom, I reach my hand into my hair and pull a few strands from the bottom of my head. Then I pluck out a hair or two from my eyebrows and examine them closely. Even though it scares me to do this and my eyebrows are getting dangerously thin, I can't seem to resist.

What is the line between normal and not normal anyway?

Shannon Riley meets us on the deck. Her brown hair is straightened and parted down the middle. Usually the first thing I notice about a person is their hair. I notice the shape, color, texture, the way it frames the face, or falls out of place, and how it shines in the light. I notice this more than a person's face or outfit or anything else.

"What's going on, girlies?" Shannon says, in her high-pitched voice.

Shannon is carrying a notice-me leather purse over her shoulder, which I immediately know she'll spend the night bragging about. Shannon invites herself to our parties, seemingly unaware that no one likes her. She laughs like a hyena and constantly talks about herself in third person.

"Look at what Shannon found," she squeals. She holds out the purse for us to admire it.

"Nice bag," Kat says, nodding in approval.

"Shannon is doing a little dance," she says, making an irritating pelvic movement. She is wearing a sundress just like Kat's, but it is an obnoxious yellow color with a white belt around the waist.

"Isn't it a knock off?" I ask, recalling Shannon had posted something online about a purchase from a fake bag website.

"Alyssa, it has the designer label and came in the mail. Where do you buy your knock-offs from? Goodwill?"

Shannon is joking, but Kat lets out a smile. She knows I am fascinated by anything that comes from the thrift store. Other people's stuff has always had this strange appeal to me.

"Vivian gets bags for me at her tradeshows," I tell her.

My current favorite is a free gift from Vivian. When she threw it in the trash I came to its rescue, washing it and taking it as my own. Sometimes I feel sorry for inanimate objects that no one cares about anymore, or imagine things are alive hurting and want to help them.

I feel especially sorry for those smashed up cars you see on the freeway on top of semi trucks, flattened and pressed together. I wonder where they go. I even wonder about trash sometimes. Where does it all go, anyway?

As Shannon shows a couple other girls her new bag, I turn to Kat. "Who invited her to my party?"

"I guess she invited herself," Kat says like it isn't a big deal. "Vivian probably saw her fake bag and escorted her in."

I remind Kat about the nickname we'd given Shannon, the animal cracker. With her high-pitched, hyena-like laugh, it's a perfect fit.

"She's kind of funny," Kat says, shrugging and then she lowers her voice. "Plus, Shannon turns sixteen next week and has a BMW convertible already. Imagine the possibilities."

All I can imagine is that hyena laugh amplified in a small space.

I scan the deck for Josh Slater and I can't help but notice my parents through the window in the dining room. I wonder how it is that my father has a girlfriend and here he is with my mother and they are having dinner and throwing this party.

I head back into the house, pretending to need to use the bathroom, but I continue to look for Josh. He has always had a place in my heart, and thanks to Kat's big mouth, I'm pretty sure he knows by now. I mean, how many girls have a crush on someone for *five years*? I am either obsessed or we are destined to be together.

After making sure Josh isn't lost in the front yard, I find Kat in the kitchen grabbing another drink.

"You'll never believe who just came through the back gate," she says.

"Josh?" I ask, hopeful.

"Nope. Steve Nolin."

She gestures out the window where Steve stands next to the cheese plate in a Hawaiian shirt. Steve is a tall skinny senior with ZERO personality, yet he is one of the most popular guys at our school. I think his status mostly comes from the fact that his great grandfather invented plastic, but who knows?

Steve doesn't say a whole lot. He pretty much towers above everyone with his mouth half open, nods a lot, and probably drools.

"I thought Steve was taking photos in Tahiti for that surfing website" I say, pointing in his direction like he is a bulls-eye. I remember seeing a few photos online, which were just as dull as Steve. There was a blurry nighttime ocean photo, one of some little waves, and a pair of birds huddled together.

Kat pushes my hand down. "Don't point at him, Alyssa. We don't want him to know we're talking about him."

"Sorry. It's not like he saw us. The guy doesn't seem to have a lot going on upstairs, if you know what I mean."

"Steve is just misunderstood."

"That's what they say about all the psychopaths."

"He wouldn't hurt a thing," Kat insists. "You don't know anything about guys anyway. You've never even had a boyfriend."

"Yeah, and I don't plan on dating Steve."

I tug on my necklace, wondering what happened to the Kat and Alyssa who used to finish each other's sentences. Lately it feels like we are banging our heads together. I don't want to state the obvious, but sometimes I think the only reason we are still friends is because we have been for so long.

I have no idea what Kat sees in Steve and as she strolls away to attempt to flirt with him, I immediately regret not insisting we invite some of my swim team friends to the party. They aren't in our crowd, but I like to hang out with them in the hot tub after practice. I like the common bond we have in the pool.

Kat jokes that the swimmers are all lesbians, so it's better to keep my distance unless I am into that kind of thing.

I hadn't bothered to defend them and tell her that even the one lesbian girl is really cool. Those friends know me in a different way. We pass each other in that quiet place under the water where everything is quiet and peaceful and okay.

chapter three

Long story short, Josh didn't come to the party to say goodbye because he broke his toe. I swear that guy always has an excuse. The evening ended with Kat and Steve kissing in the orange trees and Shannon making the announcement about her BMW-themed birthday party.

There were no tears, mentions of "I'll miss you," or long, drawn out hugs or goodbye gifts. Really it could have been a casual backyard party of any sort, which sort of bothers me.

Maybe it's not such a bad thing to be moving. Plus, I'll get a chance to stop my weird habit before it gets any worse.

The first few nights at Grandma's house, I make a vow: *I will get better here.* And at first I do, with the distractions of unpacking and the strangeness of being in a new place. My temporary bedroom is upstairs, next to the bathroom that Vivian and I share.

The bedroom is no bigger than my walk-in closet back home, barely fitting a twin-size bed and wooden dresser. The walls are painted a dramatic coral red and there are faded, pink-checkered curtains on the window.

I wonder when was the last time someone actually slept in this bed. Even though Vivian washed the sheets three times, it still smells like stale potato chips. I lie there under an old quilt wondering, what I am doing here?

I am getting to know my grandma before we destroy her home.

Instead of decorating the bedroom walls with something normal, like paintings of flowers, Grandma has a row of horse butts sewn from colorful fabric, with long tails in different colors and textures that feel like real hair. I sit up in bed and comb my fingers through one of the tails and then quickly pull my hand back.

They remind me of stuffed animals that could come alive in the night and attack you. There is a reason I banned myself from watching horror movies in the eighth grade. I immediately take the horse butts down and store them under the bed.

The house is so unlike any place I've slept before that I can't help but be distracted, with no desire to do anything bad to myself.

I even make it an entire week without pulling a single hair and wonder if I'm cured before going into the bathroom and frantically digging out the tweezers.

I pluck out all the eyebrow hairs that are "different"—ones that face the wrong direction, are a darker color, or just feel out of place to the touch. It is like a game of sorts, only I feel crazy afterward and I don't stop there. I comb through the thick hairs on my head, allowing myself to twirl a few and rub them between my fingertips.

Then I can't resist. I pull a few out, feeling a throbbing sensation that makes my eyes water, yet I want to do it again.

If Vivian, Josh, Kat, or anyone else knew what I was doing to myself, they would probably disown me. Vivian is always happy to point out my flaws, including that I need to be taller and my flat chest that hasn't got the memo about growing in yet.

Thanks, I know.

As we circle the gymnasium for orientation at my new high school, Vivian stuffs neon-colored flyers from every club under her arms, drawing attention to her perfectly round balloon-size boobs.

I am grateful she is not wearing anything too low cut today. Still, it's hard not to notice the stares she gets from my male classmates.

As the Barbie Lady, Vivian proudly details her plastic surgery ventures on the Internet for adoring fans. I don't visit her site and I hope no one at this school does either. It would be nice, for once, to just remain anonymous.

The gym is buzzing with students, some leashed to parents, other moving along like packs of wolves. I am wearing an entire wardrobe from second hand stores for this occasion. I usually save these clothes for wearing around the house, but since I don't know anyone here, and frankly don't care, I saw no need to change earlier. I know my vintage Mr. Bubbles t-shirt and orange shoelaces are a bit eccentric (and probably giving Vivian a mini heart attack), but it pleases me to dress this way.

I feel more like myself, you know?

I wouldn't dare take a fashion risk back home where the girls would raise their eyebrows at anything that isn't name brand and trendy, but here it's like an experiment. I can do whatever I want because no one knows who I am.

My hair is in a long fishtail braid and some curls fall across my face. I tuck a curl behind my ear.

"Let's go meet the cheerleaders," Vivian suggests, as we

approach their table filled with black and red pompoms. "After all, your best friend is a cheerleader. Maybe these girls will become your friends too."

I scoff at the idea.

"Did you and Kat get in a fight or something?"

"No. But we're only going to live here until December. I don't want to make any new friends, okay?"

"Oh come on," she says. "Live a little. Carpe diem. Sometimes I can't believe we're related."

"Sometimes I can't believe it either," I mutter, feeling my skin crawl. Vivian likes to insert clichés into conversation like she just invented them over coffee this morning.

Vivian and I operate in different galaxies and hers is always trying to overtake mine, Barbie style. Besides advice about my social life, she likes to give me little "gifts" from her side business, Glamour Prix Cosmetics. My personal favorite is the Glow in the Dark Elbow Exfoliant, the ideal gift for an evening power outage. Other things I am happy to take, like the mascara and eyeliner, or the lipsticks I gift to Kat.

"Good morning everyone," one of the cheerleaders says, speaking into a microphone in the center of the gym and asking the crowd to please take a seat. She is small and exotic looking, like a glass Asian doll with black and red ribbons weaving through her short, perky ponytails.

I plop my butt on the bleachers. The cheerleaders don't look very friendly with the red scorpion emblems sewn on their uniforms.

"As you all know," the girl begins, "I'm Jasmine Petrovich, sophomore class president and head cheerleader."

About seven girls in the front row whistle and cheer for

Jasmine, while the rest of the room is mostly quiet. I realize the front row is exactly where I would be sitting if I were back home. Kat always claimed the most important seats for us.

For whatever reason, I immediately don't get a good vibe from Jasmine or any one of them. From this vantage point the girls in the front row look like they are trying too hard to be hot stuff.

"She is beautiful," Vivian says, elbowing me as if I should take notes. "You should wear your hair like that some time."

In two ponytails? I'll pass. Seriously, I would get mistaken for a ten year old and have to go to therapy for the rest of my life.

I take out my phone and send a message to Kat.

How are you?

Good, but missing you! Shannon is having her b-day party next weekend. Everyone is going. Josh Loverboy too.

Kat likes to make up nicknames for Josh, teasing me about my forever crush on him.

I swear that guy avoids me on purpose, I write.

No way. I'm sure he misses you. You'll hear from him soon.

It's taking him long enough. You'll send me the party photos, right?

Definitely! I'll get one of J.L.'s luscious lips for you.

Kill me now.

"Alyssa, I think we know her," Vivian whispers, motioning toward Jasmine. "Grandma used to talk about this adopted Korean girl in her neighborhood."

I am not sure why this information is relevant, but Vivian keeps talking. "You attended Jasmine's birthday party when you were five. Do you remember?"

"No."

Dead yet? Kat writes.

"You really don't remember?" Vivian asks, disappointed.

"No," I repeat.

I have no memories before the age of six. I could have been born in the African jungle for all I know.

"Well, *I* remember Jasmine," she continues. "She has really come a long way. She barely spoke English back then."

"That's nice," I say, as Jasmine uses the words "totally rockin' insane" in a sentence.

"She'd be a great connection for you at this school."

I frown, ignoring her babble.

A trickle of laughter crosses the crowd as Jasmine holds up an airplane safety belt, buckling it and telling us this year is going to be a wild ride. I scan the crowd, looking for an escape route. Students and parents lean forward in their seats, mesmerized. Then I notice a guy perched on the top row of the bleachers.

He is watching me.

I turn away. Then I look back just to confirm I'm not hallucinating. His eyes are right on me. I feel my face turning an embarrassing shade of red.

Sometimes I get a reminder that I've never been kissed or asked out by a guy before. I know I'm only fifteen, but sometimes it feels like I am the last girl in the world.

I almost kissed Josh last year in Kat's basement, but then I nearly panicked right before it happened.

We were playing a game of "I've Never" with a few friends. Don't ask me why we were playing a dumb game like this one. You're supposed to go around in a circle and say things you have never done before. If someone else has done what you mention, they are supposed to take a drink.

When kissing was mentioned, Josh and I were the only ones who didn't take a drink.

"Come on you guys," Kat said, grabbing my arm and Josh's. "You just need to get it over with. I know you both want to. What's it going to take anyway, huh?"

Josh smiled at me and shrugged. He was so cute, with his glasses and his hair tucked behind his ears. I didn't even mind his giant forehead or the fact that he appeared to be growing a unibrow.

But I then I started to feel faint. My face and body were burning up and I was doing everything I could to not pass out.

"Hold on a minute," I said, jumping up and heading to the bathroom where I was worried I was about to have a panic attack. I'd never had one before, but it seemed completely possible that I could suddenly lose it right then and there.

I gave myself a pep talk. I just needed a little more time to warm up to the idea of kissing Josh in real time. I'd imagined our first kiss hundreds of times, but now it was happening.

This was *it*.

I came back out to the game, ready this time, but no one was sitting in the circle anymore. The game was over and forgotten—at least by everyone else.

I caught Josh's eye across the room. I couldn't tell if he was disappointed or relieved.

That night, I went home and let out a few tears when Vivian asked me about the party. I spilled my guts about how much I liked Josh and that I'd screwed everything up.

"What if it was my only chance?"

"If he likes you there will be more, sweetie."

But mostly she wanted to hear about the moment I froze up, like the rest of the story wasn't as compelling. Then she wiped my tears off my cheek and offered me a glass of wine. "Take it. It'll help you relax."

I blew my nose and sipped the wine, but it tasted like cold bubbly dish soap. I don't know how adults drink that stuff without spitting it out on the spot. "You better not put this on your website," I said to her, realizing I had probably said too much.

"I have never mentioned you on it," she said, her eyes cold again. "If you ever had surgery or wanted a makeover, that would be one thing, but I'll never mention you otherwise."

"Good," I muttered, unsettled about the idea.

I tried to forget what happened that night with Josh. I tried going on the Internet, texting Kat, and cleaning every crevice in my room—which was already cleaned thanks to Vivian's relentless scrubbing.

The only thing that calmed me down and shut off my thoughts was searching… for hairs.

Stop. Just stop it.

But I wasn't there anymore. A beautiful, peaceful rolling wave of quiet would fall over me, as if I was evaporating and there was nothing else.

Even with this problem getting worse, I still can't stop myself. And for the first time, I face the mirror the night before sophomore year starts and realize my left eyebrow is gone. It's missing completely.

I try and think of excuses:

I fell into a campfire.

My acne cream burned it off.

I used too much eyebrow wax.

I think something might be seriously wrong with me.

Instead of looking over my schedule of classes and planning my outfit for the first day of school, I do an online search on hair pulling, vowing to erase the search results.

Trick-uh-till-uh-mania: a Greek word meaning trich (hair), tillein (to pull) and maniaor (a frenzy, morbid desire).

I read the description. It fits so perfectly it's like someone took out my brain and recorded what I do to create the definition. It's strange to realize I discovered on my own what someone else hundreds of miles away was also doing, all alone and in secret.

I don't know how that is possible.

I am thankful Vivian has enough makeup kits that she'll never know if I take an eyebrow pencil and do my best to draw in what is gone on my face.

Sometimes, when I get my makeup just right I am the future girlfriend of a rock star. Other times, like first thing in the morning, I am an unmistakable future cat lady blogger.

Next I apply some of Vivian's lipstick, hoping it might plump my lips over time and decide to keep a tube for myself, trying to distract from the missing eyebrow. My hair is curled and the sun bleached curls fall over my shoulders like ocean waves crashing together.

The next morning I wake up an hour earlier than I usually do on a school day and redo my makeup.

"Alyssa," Vivian calls, from the stairs, "I'm starting the car. You don't want to be late on your first day."

"I'm coming," I say, taking one last look in the mirror.

A few minutes later I join her in the Lexus, wearing a pair of oversized sunglasses. I say a little thank you she can only see half of my face.

We drive past the Vegas strip on the freeway with billboards for casinos and strip clubs. I immediately miss the San Diego scenery of prime surfing spots and flowers that always seem to be in bloom.

I grip my bag tightly with the makeup and compact mirror inside, realizing I still haven't looked at my class schedule or the school map. It feels like I'm about to walk the plank.

chapter four

Sunset High School is a building so pasty white it is blinding under the deep blue sky. Vivian pulls up to the curb, wishing me good luck and reaches out for a hug. I don't want her face too close to mine, so I give her a weak pat on the arm and leap out of the car.

"See you after school?" I ask.

"I think so," she says. "Otherwise, I'll call if I'm going to be late."

"Sounds good," I say, shutting the door.

She waves and drives away, leaving me alone. I know I should start walking and go inside, but instead I face the school, pretending to be a tree.

What kind of tree should I be?

You know, the crooked, weird one, I hear a voice inside my head say.

I notice a palm tree with crispy, blackened leaves on one side.

Hello, Mr. Tree. I understand.

I've heard that trees can breathe. If you stare at them long enough (or do drugs like some unnamed people in my middle school), the trunk of a tree appears to move in and out.

As a swimmer I've held my breath under water, just to see how long I can go. Breathing under water is something I wish I could learn, like driving a car or doing a back flip.

One of my stranger daydreams is imagining myself sinking to the bottom of a pool after diving off the high dive and not coming back up. It is so quiet at the bottom, like you're just this ripple. I'd watch the bubbles float up under my nose, daring myself to stay down as long as possible.

I get short of breath just thinking about it.

I reach for my phone and text Kat. We haven't spoken in two days. This is the first time since kindergarten that I have started the first day of school without her.

Usually we link arms and walk into the building together.

Instead, I'm walking next to unfamiliar faces and seeing more white buildings that seem to have materialized out of nowhere after orientation. It's a good thing I'm wearing an oversized white shirt that blends me right in. I push my sunglasses up and keep my head down, allowing my hair to spill over my face.

I can smell the shampoo from this morning, a combination of green apples and ginger. I inhale the scent. It's comforting.

Somehow I find homeroom and slip into a desk near the wall. I envision my imaginary friend, Aurora Stone, strolling into the room instead of me. She immediately starts chatting with that cheerleader, Jasmine Petrovich on the opposite side of the room. They are instant friends.

My homeroom teacher, Mrs. Boyer, takes out the attendance list and asks, "Are there any students new to Clark County here today?"

I swallow, not wanting to draw attention to myself, but the guy next to me raises his hand. "Yes. Right here."

"What's your name and where are you from?"

"Alex Castillo. I'm from San Diego."

I turn toward him and freeze. He has olive skin, dark eyes, and a mass of black hair. He is dressed more formally than everyone else in a forest green button up shirt with a collar.

Something is familiar about him and then I realize what it is. He was the guy staring at me at orientation.

"Is anyone else new today?" Mrs. Boyer calls out.

I hesitate, and before I can get my hand up, she makes the announcements about school and class rules, which includes no hats or bandanas. I wonder if I'm going to get in trouble for not admitting I am new, but things move right along as if nothing out of the ordinary has happened.

I take a strand of my hair over my forehead and separate the curls. Oh well.

We are all given forms to fill out about our interests. When Alex passes a form to me he stops and asks, " So, what's the story on this school, anyway?"

I flip the strand of hair back toward my head, feeling nervous. His eyes are dark, like a good mystery, and when I gaze into them I don't want to look away.

"This place?" I say, as my brain turns into a Pop-Tart and stops working. The classes, I tell him, are okay, but we don't get enough breaks during the day. The students are your usual serving of slackers, smartys, skaters, sluts, and a kid I point out in the corner who might possibly be drunk. I don't know where these lies are coming from, but they fall right out of my lips.

"Then there are people like us," I say, stopping myself before revealing what we have in common. I ask him about his old school. He tells me a familiar name in San Diego.

"It must be nice there," I say.

"It is the best," he says with a faraway smile, and I notice he has an adorable tiny space between his front teeth. "But I don't know when I'll be back. My life is pretty complicated right now, you know?"

"I understand," I say, even though I don't.

He surveys the room again. "Do you know everyone here?"

I laugh, trying to think of an answer. "No way. I try to stay in the background. It's pretty easy."

"Why do you do that?"

"I don't know. When you move around a lot everything kind of blends together. One school after another."

"I've moved around a lot too."

"Yeah?" I squeak, hardly able to believe what I'm saying. I want this conversation to end immediately. I feel like I am reading words from a teleprompter.

Actually, I'm the daughter of a plastic surgery fanatic.

I'm here to star in a reality show at my dead grandmother's house.

I'm fifteen, but most people say I look younger.

I don't know anyone here. Except you, I think.

I lean back in my chair, hoping he won't notice my drawn-on eyebrow or how nervous I am.

"What's your name?" he asks rolling up his sleeves.

"Alyssa."

"That's a pretty name."

"Thanks. My dad liked the name Alison and my mom liked Lisa, so they combined the two names." I gesture like we're playing charades and my hand is a ceiling fan.

"I wasn't named after anyone," he says. "I was born in Mexico City and moved out here when I was a kid."

Alex proceeds to tell me his life story. It includes moving to California with his brother while his father and other siblings continued the family business in Mexico City. Then, losing the house where he was living San Diego with relatives and being shipped to Vegas to live with "crazy Uncle Ringo" for the school year.

"After that, who knows?" he says. "I just try to live one day at a time."

"Me too," I say, feeling awful about lying. I hadn't expected this conversation to last this long. I wrack my brain for what Kat would do next and start on a story about visiting Costa Rica and modeling swimsuits. I wait for him to laugh and call my bluff.

Instead he says, "Nice. You'll have to show me the photos sometime."

I blush, surprised he believes me. "Uh, I think I threw them out."

"What?! You're telling me you're a model who threw away las fotos. Estas loca."

I smile, but it's bittersweet. Vivian and my father did go to Costa Rica last year, but I stayed home with Kat's family.

"I have a good one," he says, as if we really are swapping stories. "This shark tooth on my necklace has been in my family for years."

He invites me to come closer and check out the necklace under his collar. It has a black leather cord and a shark tooth hanging from the center. I reach for it, and then pretend to cough. I don't want him to see my eyebrow too close.

"My mother battled the shark with her bare hands. Actually they killed each other. She lost so much blood that she died in the attack."

"Wow. Seriously?"

Alex nods, his eyes getting darker.

I find it hard again to look away from him. "What happened?"

"We were on vacation. My mom and me and my older brother were wading in the ocean, and then my mom was out there alone. She went in further, up to her waist and was just standing there letting the waves wash over her. That's when she was attacked. She fought back, very hard, but then the shark dragged her out to sea and she died. Just like that."

"What a nightmare. I'm so sorry."

"My brother is the one who remembers that day. I think I blocked it out."

I think of all the times I've been in the ocean, unafraid.

"It's strange too because no one in my family ever went out very far in the water. You just don't do that if you can't swim. I used to wonder if the shark was calling out to her."

"Or maybe it was a riptide?"

"Maybe. I kind of like to believe it was something supernatural."

Alex is unlike anyone I know and yet he is exactly the kind of friend I want here. Plus, I can't take my eyes off him. The more we talk the more I realize he is gorgeous.

Why did I lie earlier?

We compare schedules and see that we have lunch at separate times, but we both have fourth period P.E.

I wonder how many girls he had kissed. He seems like the kind of guy who has kissed *a lot* of girls.

For me, not having been kissed yet makes me feel like a weirdo. Sometimes I actually wonder if someone put a curse on me. I worry too that I might not get kissed in high school and then what if college comes and still no one kisses me? Then I'll be an adult and I will be really screwed.

It doesn't help that Kat texts me every time she gets kissed. She always has a name and a number, adding up each one like it's a funny game.

#17. Sexy Ben. Lifeguard at tower 5.

#18. French guy. What was his name again?

#19. Hawaiian Shirt Steve.

Sometimes I wonder if she makes up a name just to give herself more credit. More often, though, each one is a reminder of my lack of points, which is holding steady at #0.

For now.

chapter five

When the crew for *Kicking it at Grandma's House* knocks on the front door, I am the lucky one to greet them and find a camera and lights directed at me.

"You must be Alyssa," a handsome man with a strong jawbone and blue jean overalls says, reaching out to shake my hand. He has thick, sandy brown hair that is styled as if he just got out of bed.

"Vivian!" I yell, ignoring his handshake. I'm surprised she hasn't run right up to the door panting with excitement. "Is that thing on?" I ask, nodding to the camera.

"Every second," the handsome man says. "Sorry for the unannounced arrival. We like to surprise you when you're least expecting it." He nails me with an enthusiastic smile. It is a gesture that says I am supposed to recognize him and start doing a worship dance.

Instead, I give him a blank look and bite into an apple.

"Sooooo," he continues. "I'm Mighty Mike. I'm sure you recognize me from the show." He runs his hand through his signature hair, ruffling it up and smiling even bigger.

"Uh, yeah," I lie, looking from him to the silent cameraman to a skinny guy carrying a bag twice his size and an older man carrying an ax.

"Tell us what this house symbolized for your grandma."

"Your guess is as good as mine," I say, glancing around the entrance where we are standing. There are shelves filled with old books and trinkets like stuffed barnyard animals, holiday decor, an old typewriter, and a strange sculpture made out of milk jugs that looks like an insect.

I realize I have no idea where the camera lens might be focusing and I haven't redone my makeup since this morning. I quickly grab the oversized sunglasses out of my bag.

"Oh, you don't have to wear those," Mighty Mike says. "We know these lights are killer bright. You'll get used to them in a few minutes."

"They are pretty bright," I agree, shading my face with my hand. "I think protective eyewear is necessary."

"I like it," he says. "You've got some attitude. Put that microphone on her pronto."

"How long are you filming?" I ask, as the skinny guy hands me a tiny microphone to hide under my shirt.

"We'll be here for the next four months. You know how it all works, right?"

"You're going to make some home improvements, right?"

"You might say that," Mighty Mike says with a chuckle. "Didn't you see the contract?"

I shake my head.

"Yikes, don't tell the production crew." He slugs the guy behind him. "That could be illegal. You're not eighteen, are you, darling?"

"No, I'm fifteen," I say dryly, knowing I don't look a day older.

"Here's how it works. Basically, we're going to demolish the house while you live here."

The guy carrying an ax adds, "It'll be epic."

"That's the beauty of the show. Not only does the house transform, but the people inside get to enjoy it every step of the way." Mighty Mike reaches for one of Grandma's stuffed roosters near the front door. "Let's just say this stuffed animal will also transform."

"He means we're going to be decapitating stuffed animals," the ax guy says.

"Don't worry," I say. "I don't sleep with my teddy bear anymore."

Vivian steps into the room on cue with her phone pressed to her ear and a martini in her hand. She is wearing a flower print body-hugging dress that shows off every curve and then some. She waves the crew toward her. They follow like hungry dogs.

"This must be your older sister," Mighty Mike says, salivating. "Sweet."

"Actually, I'm an only child," I respond automatically, before realizing he is joking.

Vivian's face and body are made for the camera. *Literally*. Her skin is tight and her features symmetrical. She has a kind of beauty that is almost out of this world. It makes you want to look at her harder, just to see if you can find the flaws.

You *can* find flaws, but in photos or video of her she really does resemble a doll. Or at least someone is who trying to look like one.

She is mostly known for her boob job and perfect proportions, not to mention the endless work on her nose and cheek implants and other stuff I've lost track of. As she leans toward the camera with delight, I make a mental note to buy some more padded bras ASAP.

Her "before" photos are displayed in fancy frames in the kitchen, like the one from her senior year, where her unremarkable face and nose and body are shaped just like mine.

"You can visit Dr. Pang when you're old enough," she tells me from time to time. "I know you don't want to be a doll, but your nose could be smaller and your chin less pointy, and a few other things you already know about."

"Okay," I tell her weakly, not liking when Vivian stares at me, probably surgically enhancing me with her eyeballs. Sometimes she watches me like a hawk, even if we're just in front of the TV. The last thing I want to do is transform into her when I grow up.

Mighty Mike explains he'd like to set up an informal interview in the kitchen. He scans the barnyard wallpaper, orange curtains made pale by decades of sunlight, and a groaning pea-green refrigerator with an array of mismatching coffee mugs on top.

"Why are you wearing sunglasses?" Vivian asks.

"My eyes hurt," I respond, briskly opening the curtains.

Mighty Mike asks us to pose behind of the kitchen counter. A couple of the crew members approach and apply a dust of makeup over our faces. Or, in Vivian's case, I should say more makeup. I stare at the rows of wallpaper cows across the kitchen, praying no one says anything about my eyebrow, or how ordinary I am.

I fluff up the back of my curly hair and adjust the sunglasses, realizing we're about to start filming again in a more formal way.

"I hear that Grandma had a clutter problem," Mighty Mike says as the camera rolls again.

"Yes," Vivian answers solemnly. "I can hardly move in here without knocking over her junk. One of my personal favorites is the piggy platter." She holds up a glass platter shaped as a pig with two black dots for eyes. "Oink, oink."

"And that's where we come in," Mighty Mike says, with a booming voice, stepping between us. He puts his arms around us like we're old friends. "Is there anything you want to salvage? Any treasures lost in the roughage?"

"Nope," Vivian says flatly. "We don't want any of it."

"Excellent! That means we're going to be painting, knocking out walls, auctioning off these knickknacks." He gestures at a giant, decorative wooden fork, spoon, and knife hanging on the wall. "Anybody know a giant who needs utensils? Text me, baby."

He takes out his phone, pointing to it playfully.

I frown, thinking that even though I didn't know Grandma, auctioning off her stuff in such a public display is a bit much.

Mighty Mike continues. "We may find some lost treasures and as you viewers at home know, they will be displayed on our website. So, if you want a little piece of this old school grandma, you know where to click."

He turns to me. "What would your grandma say about all this cleaning?"

"I don't know. It seems kind of invasive. Maybe she liked her stuff, even if it's junk."

"Cut!" the skinny guy yells.

I am given a lecture from the crew on the importance of being upbeat and positive. I suddenly feel like a child getting reprimanded for misbehaving, something I rarely remember even when I was little.

"Alyssa," Vivian says. "Can you agree to be positive and friendly on the show?"

"Yes," I say, but it all seems so fake to me.

The cameraman signals he is ready to start filming again and this time he focuses on Vivian and Mighty Mike.

"I hear you have a special nickname," Mighty Mike says.

"Yes, the Barbie Lady," Vivian says proudly. "You might say it's my claim to fame."

"Folks, we may be doing more than just a home makeover this season."

"You'll have to wait and see," Vivian says with a wink.

"Are you ready to start this thing?" Mighty Mike yells, handing Vivian and me safety goggles and hammers.

"Yes!" we say in unison, just like we've been told.

"Then let's show this house we mean business." The three of us march off camera toward the living room.

"That's a wrap," the skinny guy says.

About thirty seconds later they are out the door.

I look at Vivian, "Well, that was interesting."

A few days later Vivian carries a stack of binders out to the Lexus, balancing in her very high heels down the driveway. She is in charge of promoting the Del Sol Grand Resort, a new upscale hotel, casino, and spa.

"When will you be home?" I ask.

"Around ten."

I groan, hating the thought of being alone here after dark. Sometimes I worry when I'm alone what might happen. Like, say I suddenly couldn't breathe, or my lungs couldn't pump the air properly, or if my heart stopped beating all of a sudden.

I know I shouldn't, but sometimes I worry about stuff like this.

Most of Grandma's stuff hasn't been touched, although the floors, dishes, furniture and towels have all been washed twice over. This is part of the agreement for the show. I know the rest must be torture for Vivian, who is meticulous to the tiniest dust bunny.

She especially hates dirty carpet. If things went her way, we'd all just float over the carpet, keeping the vacuum lines crisp.

The worst part of the junk museum is Grandma's life-size statues, including ones of painted cats. Some are curled up in the hallway, some stand guard, and some gaze out at nothing. I swear their black eyeballs follow me sometimes.

I already have this irrational fear that one might come to life and bite me. Cats are scary and unpredictable like that.

"Can you help me carry the rest of these folders to the car?" Vivian asks sweetly, handing me a stack.

I follow her out to the driveway and she sticks her head inside the trunk, mumbling something about Jasmine Petrovich, the head cheerleader.

"Have you made any friends here yet?"

"Not really."

"No one?" she says, sounding disappointed. "It's been a few weeks."

"Well, I did meet this guy. He's really interesting. He was born in Mexico."

"Well, don't forget about Jasmine. We could host a party and invite her and some other girls to come over. Maybe they'd want to make an appearance on the show with you. Wouldn't that be fun?"

"Maybe." I hesitate thinking about my last party. "Let me

think about it," I say, before she runs off and starts planning.

Vivian steps past me, shuffling back up the driveway. "What about swim team? When is your first practice?"

"I'm not on the team yet," I say quickly.

"I thought you had practice on Thursdays."

"I do, but I pulled this muscle in my shoulder. Ouch."

I move my left shoulder, trying to convince myself that it hurts. Vivian has no idea I avoid the water now like it has a disease. I go into the pool area and spend an hour on the bleachers watching the swimmers do their drills and biting my fingernails hoping that no one notices me.

"The coach says I should stay out for the rest of the year," I add.

"The whole *year*? Why didn't you say something earlier? It's your only extracurricular talent."

I shrug, trying not to look too guilty. "I'll find something else to do."

What I really want to say is that I don't want to magnify the odd things I am doing to myself. When my face gets wet, it's harder to hide the damage. I have been drawing on one eyebrow and plucking all the hairs out of the other one, just to make them match. I keep restraining from pulling fistfuls of head hair, but it's harder, as if there is a tick crawling underneath my scalp.

The human head has about 100,000 hairs (or so says Google), so I should have some time to get this thing under control. At least that is what I tell myself when I am thinking clearly. Removing a few now and then isn't a big deal. Plus, a lot of people remove a hair or two just to check them out, right?

"Thanks for the help," Vivian says, giving me money to order pizza. She kisses me on the cheek as I pull away. "Be good, Lissy. Maybe consider giving Jasmine a call. I'll bet she would help you learn the ropes here."

Instead, I wave goodbye and decide to snoop through Grandma's stuff. In a big cupboard in the living room I find dozens of plastic containers filled with colorful beads, costume jewelry, and wire. I pull each one out, putting my share into a shoebox. Mighty Mike isn't going to auction everything in this house away.

I know how to make earrings and necklaces, twisting wire and adding crystals and gemstones to my creations. I can create shapes out of the wire, as if I'm putting a puzzle together.

Once I get bored of going through Grandma's stuff, I turn on the TV and sink into the weathered La-Z-Boy chair she is said to have passed away in, flipping channels and playing with the settings on my phone. I find Josh's old text messages and read them. I write him a quick message just to say hello. I edit the text about a hundred times and then finally push send.

Now it's 11:45 and I've heard nothing from Josh or Vivian. It's one thing in San Diego where I have Kat's house as a sleepover option, but another to be here in a strange city. I suddenly wonder if Vivian is going to leave me here the whole night.

I draft a few texts asking where she is, and then I send one that I know will get a response.

My stomach hurts.

This isn't a good time for you to be sick, she responds. *I'm still working.*

When will you be home?

Later. Just relax. Okay? You can put yourself to bed, right?

What about my stomach ache?

I'll get you something on the way home.

I don't actually have a stomach ache, although if you concentrate hard enough you can force stomach pains. Getting sick usually makes her come home early and worry about me. I've made up ailments big and small—toothaches, cough, nausea, sore throats, migraines, allergies, something in the air, you name it.

I've even swallowed medications that I don't need. I never take anything too risky, just cough syrup or ibuprofen and chewable tablets for upset stomachs.

Sometimes I even secretly wish for a terrible accident.

Maybe something that would leave me in a coma. I imagine Vivian coming by daily and leaving flowers on the nightstand. She would mention me in her blog and give updates on my status, rather than her stupid plastic surgery secrets. Or maybe she would create a new blog and name it after me.

If I was in a coma I could make up the characters, the scenarios, and the world I want. I could be my imaginary friend Aurora Stone, or I could watch her from a cave, controlling every action and word out of her mouth. I could be the director of all the chaos, except I could just sit back and watch, pushing erase, fast forward, and rewind.

I would fast forward the boredom and pause at those precious moments where the sun lines up just right and the perfect guy cups my face for a kiss.

If I get too overwhelmed, I can press the Off button and take a break. That is sort of what my pulling is like, pressing Off. Again and again and again.

Everything else just melts away.

chapter six

Every day I look forward to homeroom. I actually get butterflies in my stomach when Alex walks inside. He's always wearing a different colored button up shirt with a collar, jeans, and red sneakers with black trim. He has gel in his hair today, making it extra shiny.

When he sits down beside me, I'm always surprised, even after weeks of seeing him do this. After my massive crush on Josh, who I've been chasing all these years, it amazes me that it could possibly be easier.

"Attention, everyone, I have an announcement," Mrs. Boyer says as soon as Alex sits down and gives me his usual smile with the cute, imperfect space between his teeth. "All of the new students are transferring to a special homeroom class."

I glance at Alex and frown, starting to get out of my seat and then I realize I haven't told anyone I'm new. He shrugs his shoulders and gets escorted out of the room.

My heart sinks. I haven't bothered to get to know anyone else in this class, let alone my new school. With Kat back home, I could always count on her to invite me to parties and keep me in the loop. It's harder to be on my own. I don't know how to make my own friends without her.

Jasmine and a couple other girls are chatting together in the opposite corner of the room. I make a mental note that maybe I should approach them sometime, just to see what happens. And then I see out the window that Alex is in front of the school with a group of kids near a row of cactus, and I wish I were there too.

Sometimes I just don't know how to open up my mouth and say what I want.

I take my phone out of my backpack, hiding it under the desk.

Have you kissed Steve again? I text to Kat.

She immediately writes back, *No, I'm over him.*

What happened?

He's a dud. Plain and simple. You were right.

He is pretty boring.

By the way, did you see the photos from Shannon's BMW party?

I click the link Kat gives me and browse photos from back home. I feel like I should be in these photos too and I search, but can't find myself. Instead, Shannon has managed to get herself (and her newest fake bag) into every shot.

I suddenly miss everything about home. The ocean air and sunsets. Kat and her welcoming family. Green plants. Organic food. My sometimes superficial group of friends. Even Shannon and her squeaky, annoying voice.

Then I see a photo with Kat laying across the hood of a BMW with a bikini under a shirt that is super low cut. A couple random guys have written comments underneath.

Gorgeous! I give you a 10.5.

Perfect girl.

When am I taking you out?!?

And then my eyes zero in on one that says, *Hey KitKat! Lookin' good!*

Josh's name is next to it.

Really? Is there no one who is immune to Kat's growing list of admirers? I immediately put my phone away.

Why you can't just shut your feelings off when you like someone and they don't like you back? How is that helpful evolution-wise?

I close my eyes, glancing at the clock in homeroom, and let myself have a fifteen-minute nap.

I don't fall asleep, but I do allow myself to daydream and go into the place in my mind where everything is good and right.

I imagine that I am on the front porch of a blue Victorian house where Aurora is sitting on a porch swing with her boyfriend, Hoffman. The home is surrounded by farmland and tall swaying grass. It is nighttime and the dark countryside is romantic and mysterious.

"What is love?" Aurora asks as they sit and rock together.

"Love is something you breathe in and out," her boyfriend says.

Aurora puts her head on his shoulder.

"When love is right, it's easy," he adds, taking her hand. "But you have to be careful. If you take in too much at once, you'll choke. Or if you hold your breath, it might pass you right by."

I envy Kat and all of her boyfriends and her stories about potential boyfriends. I wish the stories were mine, but I have no idea how she does it. It seems like such a huge responsibility to belong, in a way, to someone.

What if you fell in love and it died?

What if you tried, but your heart just wouldn't open?

It amazes me that this goes on every day, that people are falling in love at times, and leaving it behind at other times. It all seems so complicated and impossible to figure out with another, unpredictable person by my side.

I want to fall in love, yet it feels like a mystery, something that happens inside other people's minds and bodies. I am afraid that I will screw it up by doing, thinking or making some gesture that is wrong. Or, that he will try to run his fingers through my hair while I turn away, trying to savor the moment and hold it off just one more second.

Alex strolls into my chemistry class that day and slips into the desk next to mine. His shirt has a few buttons undone and I can see the leather cord on the shark tooth necklace.

I pretend not to care he is next to me all of a sudden, but I am totally nervous. To distract myself, I focus on drawing square-shape swirl symbols on my ankle with a purple jelly pen. We are supposed to be working in study groups to memorize the periodic table, but there is a substitute teacher today and most people are socializing

"I missed you," Alex says, leaning into my desk so only I can hear him.

I freeze for a second and then lift my head and respond, "Oh sure."

My legs are tucked under each other, the purple pen pressed to my skin. I am small and very flexible, so it's easy for me to sit this way, like a human pretzel.

"I'm serious," he says, watching me with those dark amazing eyes. "I think it's cool you can sit like that. How do you do it?"

"Magic," I answer with a smile. "Why are you in this class today?"

"Magia," he answers back. "Actually, I was in an AP chemistry class with a bunch of seniors. I tried to stick with it and get college credits, but I got outed. At least I held on for a few weeks."

"That's impressive. You must be really smart."

"I try hard," he says, with a chuckle.

"How was your new homeroom?" I ask.

"It was okay. We mostly sat outside passing a jar of olives around a circle." He leans forward, checking out the drawing on my ankle. "I'm still recovering from a bad 'getting to know you' game."

"Well, did you get to know anyone?"

"No one as interesting as you," he says, taking my pen and adding a diamond shape on my ankle.

"You're funny. You know that?"

I feel a little sick at the thought of the tall tales I've told him and figure we should probably stop getting to know each other right about now. I take the pen from him, putting my head down and coloring one of the swirls into a square box.

"What all are you doing there?" he persists.

"I like to decorate myself."

"You should get a tattoo like that some day. I know a guy who can hook you up."

"I can't get a tattoo."

"Why not?"

"I don't know. Needles scare me."

"What's wrong with needles?"

"They're needles. They hurt."

"Don't be a needle hater. How do you know they hurt, anyway?"

"I can imagine it," I say.

Alex gives me a weird look and then glances back at his desk. "Not everything bad you imagine will turn out that way."

"Actually, if you really want to know, I'll tell you the reason." I lower my voice so no one else can hear me. "I keep having this dream where I am in the hospital and they are going to stick hundreds of giant needles into me. Like, they have a conveyer belt and you can see each one lined up with deadly liquid inside."

I pause, realizing I am about to reveal to Alex something I've never told anyone before. "I've never had any vaccinations. No shots ever. My parents didn't want me to get them. They don't believe in it."

"Wow. Crazy."

"I think my mom might be crazy, actually. For real."

"Most people are a little crazy."

"Some more than others. You haven't met my mom."

"Shouldn't you be dead by now from the measles or something?"

"Probably," I say, realizing I really could catch something right at this moment and die.

"That's all the more reason to get a tattoo."

"Why is that?"

"You're not dead yet."

"True." It is a freaky thought.

"Before I die," Alex says, "I am going to get a tattoo. Hopefully I'll be getting it very soon."

"Because you're going to die?"

"No, because I want a tattoo, silly."

Alex digs around in his backpack and pulls out a piece of paper

57

with an image he sketched of a cross between a Chinese dragon and a snake. It's in an "s" shape, with fire coming out of the mouth and the tail tucked into a square-shaped spiral. The spirals I'd drawn on my ankle are eerily similar to the creature's tail.

"You're a good artist," I say. "What kind of animal is it exactly?"

"It's a serpent. There are carvings of this on ancient ruins in South America. It feels like this creature runs in my blood."

"You're lucky," I say. "You know where you belong."

"Not really. I just want to honor where I came from."

I think about how Alex is so worldly and interesting and all these things that feel opposite from me. "I'd like to travel more," I say. "Then maybe I'd know where I belong, too."

"Isn't half of the world enough for you?"

I swallow, remembering my Costa Rica travel story. "I forget sometimes."

Alex smiles, his dark eyes melting into mine. I avert my gaze, kind of hoping he'll do the same. It feels like he can see right into me, right into my deepest and darkest thoughts.

The bell rings and I am relieved to end this conversation.

It's lunchtime, the worst part of the day. I still haven't figured out what to do with myself or how to make friends. You always see those movies where the new girl gets rescued when she needs it most in the cafeteria. Of course, those movies never show you what happens before the rescue attempt.

They don't show you the bathroom stall where that girl has been hiding and playing with her phone. At least I've found a pattern. I usually walk as slow as possible, eating my homemade bagel sandwich, which takes about seven minutes. Then I slip into the bathroom, taking the rear stall next to a window and send texts to Kat.

Sometimes she writes back, sometimes I hear nothing and play Tetris on my phone instead. I like when we joke around like old times and gossip about people in our class. I don't like when she is busy with her stupid games.

#20, Matt behind the parking lot.

What! I write back. *Aren't you still with Steve?*

I thought I told you already. We broke up.

When?

Last week.

Ugh! Sorry, I lost track.

It's fine. I'm having fun.

What about you? Any guys? Or still hung up on Joshy Pants?

Josh is my soul mate. You know that.

I know, I know. But maybe there is someone else out there?

Just one. This guy Alex. He's cute.

Text me his photo, she writes.

I'll try.

It's time for lunch. Matt asked me to sit with him. Gotta run.

Got a new friend too, I respond. *Jasmine is waiting for me.*

I glance in the mirror, annoyed with how Kat goes through guys like they are disposable objects. My hair looks good today, with the curls framing my face. I try not to look too close at my eyebrows or lashes, which are not so hot lately.

Then I exit the bathroom and grab a bag of chips from the vending machine. The cafeteria area is right outside and packed with people.

Jasmine and her clan are sitting in the center at a concrete picnic table. When I see Jasmine get up and walk over alone to the concession stand, I put on my best game face and follow her.

"Hey," I say, as she stops in front of a window, ordering a drink. I wonder if she recognizes me from homeroom. "So, I guess we used to know each other a long time ago."

She stares at me with her almond-shaped eyes, snapping a piece of gum through her front teeth. Her skin is pale and so clear. She has, what I see up close, some of the most perfectly shaped eyebrows I have ever seen. And there is not a trace of zits on her chin.

I ramble on, thinking about my imperfections.

Jasmine's head, which is a little too large for her body, tilts like her neck is fastened on wrong. Then I realize she has a headphone in one of her ears.

Stupid me.

She pulls it out. "Are you talking to me?"

"Yeah," I say, hesitating. "We knew each other in kindergarten. You live near my grandmother's house. Actually she's not there anymore, but that's where she used to live."

Jasmine continues to stare at me like I've just told her I'm from Jupiter and want her to come check out the atmosphere.

"I guess you don't remember," I continue.

"Remember what?"

"I thought maybe I could sit with you at lunch…" My voice trails off. "But never mind."

"You talk weird."

"That's okay. I didn't want to sit with you anyway," I say, and whip around to find the nearest emergency exit.

"Wait," Jasmine calls out. "We sit over there." She points to the small table. "Come join us, if you want."

I follow her once again, careful with my steps.

Don't. Fall. Down.

"Hi girls," Jasmine says and I realize there is only one chair up for grabs.

I smile sheepishly, grabbing a chair from another table and trying to scoot into a ten-inch space between Jasmine and a girl with tight curly dark hair pulled up on one side and long earrings in the shape of giraffes.

All of the girls at this table have particularly beautiful hair.

I take the bag of chips out of my bag and try to open it gracefully, but the bag makes a loud popping sound. I try to think of what Kat would say in this situation and then I imagine Aurora Stone there instead of me, joining the conversation with everyone like synchronized musical notes.

"I'm in your homeroom," I explain to Jasmine, swallowing one of the chips and feeling it scrape against my throat.

"Oh, right," Jasmine says, taking a gulp of her soda and giving me a weak smile.

Another girl I recognize from homeroom, with silky reddish hair, turns to me. "Which junior high did you come from? I don't recognize you."

"I'm not from around here," I say.

"You're not?" the girl asks, confused. "Aren't you supposed to be in that special class?"

I feel like an idiot. "Mrs. Boyer wanted me to stay in our class instead."

Jasmine turns to me again and explains how debate club needs more members and that I should join. I almost interrupt her to say I'm not interested in that kind of thing until I realize the reason she is asking is because they won't get funding if they can't recruit more people.

"I'll think about it."

"Well, if you change your mind, there's a sign up sheet by the front entrance." She turns to the red head and whispers something in her ear. I feel like I've just been axed out of the conversation and deemed useless.

The curly dark-haired girl, whose name I learn is Nicole, speaks up to the group, making eye contact with everyone except me. "So, about this party."

Right away I am lost in a sea of names and logistics, which include whether or not to invite seniors, and whether or not they will come if invited by sophomore girls, or if some of the junior girls should invite them instead.

Clearly, the question is not about whether to invite me.

I suddenly have a flash of memory about a time when one of my swim team friends sat with Kat and our group at lunch. She tried to be friendly and make conversation, but it flatlined. No one said a word to her, not even me.

chapter seven

The next day at lunch, I can't bear to hang out in the bathroom any longer. I remember the first instinct I had at this school—to do my own thing. I don't need to climb the social ladder here. In fact, I'm better off on the fringes. It's new territory.

With this thought, I take myself outside and sit on the concrete steps, noticing the mountains and red rocks in the distance. This place is definitely not home and never will be, but maybe it's a place where I can experiment. Like, I can make friends with the kind of girls Vivian doesn't approve of and who Kat would turn her nose up against. Girls like my swim team friends.

At least those girls aren't anything like Jasmine, who conveniently forget about you if you aren't of use to them.

My phone indicates a text and I see Josh's name. I smile, unable to help myself. Apparently someone hasn't forgotten me.

Hi Alyssa! I can't believe you are really gone! I'm sorry I missed your party!!!

It's good to hear from you, I write. *How did you break your toe?*

Tripped over a garden hose! Classy, huh?

You're so clumsy. Sounds like you.
I know! Nothing has changed around here!
I miss you. Text me more later, okay?
Miss you too!!! Will do!

It cracks me up that Josh ends every sentence with an exclamation point and that he continues to be a total klutz, but that's why I like him. He is funny and sweet and nerdy. I write back, telling him how great it is to hear from him and we make small talk for a few minutes.

I notice a girl from my P.E. class walking toward me; something about her tells me she is nice. She has straight brown hair that is parted in the middle like Shannon Riley. It brushes the tops of her shoulders, but unlike Shannon she is carrying a bag that looks homemade with different fabrics sewn on it.

I smile and she smiles back. To my surprise, she walks all the way to the steps. I am sitting on the top level of a cement pit with wide staircases on all four sides and a grassy area in the middle.

"Hey," she says. "You're in my P.E. class, right?"

She introduces herself as Rachel Carmichael, vegetarian, and lover of all things Australian, except the beer, which she says tastes too bitter.

"You shouldn't hang out here," she explains. "Trina Gabel became the school slut after hanging out in the pit."

I can't imagine myself *ever* being a slut, but I take Rachel's advice and stand up. She goes on to explain that Trina, who now goes to Perkins, the alternative high school, ended up with triplets that got shipped to Kentucky. "I don't even know if the whole thing is true, but it was the biggest news of the year, even at our middle school."

"Thanks for letting me know."

"You're welcome. I have to say that I don't recognize you. Are you from around here?"

I feel relief at not lying and explain that I'm living at my deceased grandmothers house and disinfecting it.

"That's a lot of Lysol," a guy standing behind Rachel says.

She introduces me to Asher Erickson, who is tall and skinny and wearing a death metal t-shirt and his girlfriend, Toni Stafford, who is short and curvy and wearing a black and white polka-dotted dress with white gloves. They are the most usual couple.

Asher shows me a piece of garlic bread that he has carved into a face. "It's my claim to fame," he says. "I make lunch art."

"Nice," I say. "So, my claim to fame is I'm on a reality show."

"What?!" All three of them say in unison.

"Well, it sounds more interesting than it actually is. I have Mighty Mike from the show *Kicking it at Grandma's House* hosting the makeover."

Everyone is impressed with my TV stardom, except that no one has actually heard of the show.

"They're not going to film you at school, are they?" Rachel asks.

"I hope not. Unless they are thinking of knocking down walls around here. I definitely don't want the attention."

"Man, you're so lucky," Toni chimes in. "Asher and I have been trying to make some episodes of a show to go viral on YouTube, but so far we only have thirty-five views."

"Thirty-*six*," Asher says.

"What is your show about?"

"My lunchtime creations," Asher says proudly. "Or sometimes we film little green soldiers in combat."

"We also have a slasher video of Asher murdering my old Barbie dolls," Toni says. "It took a lot of ketchup to make it look authentic."

"That sounds fun," I say, liking these friends already.

We walk under a grove of palm trees and everyone sits. Rachel recites some more fun facts about Sunset High, and shows me a bunch of patches from her oversized bag, each one from a different country.

"I haven't been to Australia yet," she says. "But I order these patches online and make myself a world traveler."

"Not to mention get Australian beer," Asher says.

"Oh, you can buy that anywhere," Rachel says, handing me her giant bag to check out. I flip it over, noticing about ten sewn-on patches.

"Is this handmade?" I ask.

"Yes," she says. "I made it in sewing class last year."

"I love it," I say, admiring the stitching and mismatched fabrics.

"Thanks. The best thing about it is I got all the fabric by reusing old bags," Rachel explains. "Did you know if you put all the old clothing in the whole world together, it would cover the size of Rhode Island?"

"That's a lot of clothes," I say.

"I heard the same thing about hair," Asher says.

"What?" Rachel asks.

"*Hair*," Asher repeats, emphasizing the word. "If you took all the hair in the world and made it into a visual it would cover the size of Rhode Island."

"Eww. Asher, that is the weirdest thing that has ever come out of your mouth."

"Why, thank you," he responds. "My daily goal is weirdness."

Toni leans over and kisses him on the cheek.

I look away, trying act like this lighthearted banter doesn't bother me. But the comment makes me feel uncomfortable in a way I can't explain.

I feel exposed.

After school, I stay late, waiting for Vivian, who is on her way back from a meeting and running behind, as usual. The hallways are quiet and I decide to decorate my locker. I open the gray metal door and run my finger down the ledge of the shelf to find tape and an envelope.

Inside the envelope I pull out a collection of beach photos from the summer. There's a shot of Kat posing in her silver bikini with her hands on her hips, and me next to her in a polka-dotted one. My shoulders bend inwards and hands clasp together, like I'm making an apology. Then there's a photo of us doing cartwheels in the sand and lying side by side staring up at the sky. I can almost hear her voice through the photos.

I suddenly realize Kat and I resemble each other. I don't know if I've ever noticed it before. Our smiles are the same and we both have pretty hair and slender builds, except one of us (me) looks like she would rather be crouched behind the nearest patch of seaweed. It's strange, almost like if I stood up straighter, it might wash Kat right away.

She keeps mentioning Josh in her texts, keeping me updated.

We had the annual beach bonfire with the gang. Josher brought the s'mores.

Then we talked about you all night.

Is that right? I thought. Or was it more like *We talked all night?*

I find an older photo from the sixth grade with our arms around each other in front of the San Diego zoo. It was from a field trip day. I put it back in the envelope.

"Hey you," a male voice says from behind.

Startled, I grip the locker door and whirl around to find Alex and his dark penetrating eyes. "How long have you been there?" I ask.

"Long enough."

"What do you mean?" I ask, still startled.

"I'm kidding," he says, putting a hand on my shoulder. "Relax."

Feeling his warm touch pretty much does the opposite.

"What are you doing here so late?" I ask nervously, putting the photos away. We're pretty much the only ones left in the hallway.

"I missed the bus," Alex says, leaning his arm against the locker next to mine, which nicely shows off his bicep." Plus, I saw this cute girl standing alone."

I wonder if he is joking and wait for the punch line. Then Alex doesn't say anything else and the moment fizzles. Actually, it kind of feels like someone has slapped me in the face, but in a good way, if that is possible.

"Is that your older sister?" he asks, reaching out for my locker door and opening it.

"No, she's my friend from San Diego."

"San Diego? Really? Who is she?"

I shut the door hard. "She's no one. I really need to get going. I think my ride is here already."

Amazingly, my phone rings at that instant and Vivian's name is on caller ID.

68

"Let's talk later. My mom is outside."

I pick up the phone, praying he doesn't follow me, and wind around a corner, heading toward the parking lot. My voice must sound a little too excited because Vivian says, "You sound great. What happened to you?"

"Nothing," I say. "I'm just making some friends."

"Oh good! Did you talk to Jasmine yet?"

"I did," I say.

"And was I right?"

"Yes, she is exactly like I thought she would be."

"Great. I'm glad you're getting to know her."

"So are you out front?" I ask, scanning the parking lot, my heart sinking when I don't see her car in the usual spot.

"Sorry sweetie, I'm still in meetings and I have to do a phone thingy with your dad later. But I sent over Frankie, the architect from the show to pick you up in a blue pickup truck."

"Oh, okay," I say, spotting the truck in the distance.

"Also, I have some news."

I brace myself. You never know what kind of bombs Vivian is going to drop.

"I'm going on a hot date tonight."

"A date? With who?"

"Mighty Mike asked me out. I know it sounds strange with me being married and all and us being on the show together, but he's a hottie. I wanted to tell you, rather than try to hide it."

"Did you tell Dad yet?"

"No. I doubt he would mind, though. He has that skanky girlfriend and all."

I really wish she wasn't unloading this on me over the phone, but I don't know why I would expect anything less.

At least we're not having this conversation on camera.

Frankie in the blue truck waves at me. He is wearing a big ball cap and is the oldest member of the crew, probably in his 60s. I like Frankie. I already know he'll drive me home quietly, without any interrogation.

"One more thing," she adds. "I think you should find a boyfriend too. Wouldn't it be fun if we both had boyfriends here in Vegas?"

"Are you drunk or something?" I say, half joking.

"No, Lissy," Vivian says, exasperated. "Carpe diem, remember? I know you're boy crazy even if you won't admit it."

"Carpet diem," I repeat in monotone.

"I thought you were mature enough to know what's really going on. Otherwise, I would have just lied about it."

"No, no, I want to hear everything," I say, with a bit of discomfort. "Please tell me."

"All right," she says. "Mighty Mike and I are meeting at Caesars Palace for a rendezvous. I'll be home at midnight, just like Cinderella."

"That sounds kind of romantic."

"It does, doesn't it?" I can hear the smile in her voice. "Just think, you and me can dish about guys together now. You can tell me about your conquests and I can tell you about mine."

"You already know everything," I say, referring to Josh. "And I wouldn't call it a conquest. More like a long slow uprising that never gets off the ground."

"There are many fish in the sea. Maybe you'd get noticed if you did something different with your hair. Men are attracted to ladies with shiny hair, you know? I read somewhere it's the number one thing."

"My hair?" I say, my voice nearly choking. "What's wrong with it?"

"Nothing, sweetie. Don't take everything so personally. I just want you to know that if you want a makeover while we're in Vegas, take the opportunity. I can schedule you a cut and color. You don't have to hear it from me. I think you'd look divine as a platinum blonde. It would brighten your skin and make you just pop on camera."

"Is that all you have to say on the subject?"

"What else do you want me to say?"

I want you to say that I look different lately.

"My ride is here," I respond quickly, stepping up to the truck. "Talk to you later."

I desperately want to tell someone and figure out how to stop this problem, but I find myself staying quiet day after day. Instead, I read stories online from others who say what I cannot.

I dream about the hair. I loathe the hair. I love the hair.

I wish it would never grow back and I wish it would grow back faster.

I mainly pull my eyebrows and lashes, but lately there is this tingle on my scalp.

I spend time online researching while Vivian is on her hot date. My back is against the wall as I sit up in bed, my hair in a bun off my face and my laptop sprawled out in front of me.

I've been pulling since I was a teenager, almost thirty years. I wear a wig now, one woman writes.

71

It's not a big deal anymore. The worst part is when first you try on wigs and everyone thinks you are going through chemo. Doing the damage yourself doesn't offer up as much sympathy.

Some stories are more inspiring.

Pull free thirty-one days and counting, writes one person.

I have trouble knowing what to do with my hands, writes another. *I started knitting and have twelve blankets now. Baby shower, anyone?*

It's an addiction. You're addicted to a drug, and it stares you in the face.

It lives on your body.

Another person writes, *I can't read a book or go online without doing it at the same time. Can anybody relate?*

I can, I think. *I'm doing it as we speak.*

Yikes.

I run my fingers over the bare spot behind my ear, liking the smoothness.

I recognize that tingle on the top of my scalp, too, that itch under the skin, that sensation that beckons some relief. It is maddening.

Following suggestions to try relaxing and creative visualization, I turn off the light and close my eyes and push the computer away. I count from one to ten with each exhale, trying to picture being calm and in control like Aurora Stone and finding my inner sanctuary.

I am under the ocean and rays of sunlight are shimmering like pieces of stained glass. I am a mermaid teasing the sun. Bubbles under my nose, I am just this point of movement. I am free. I am smiling at the daylight and kicking my fins under the surface and there is nothing left to hide.

Watching hair moving gracefully underwater is one of the most peaceful things I can imagine. It moves like a jellyfish. The grace and flow of this delicate thing forming different shapes: a halo, a luminous cloud, a mysterious sea creature.

I try to visualize my peaceful place, but it doesn't last long. My thoughts go in every direction at once, a living container of a gazillion random images and voices. When I pull, everything shifts into compartments where a thought gets brighter and holds steady for a moment and then disappears like a wave.

Three minutes.

I'm just going to do it for three minutes and then I'll stop.

Everything feels so clear, like all the junk in my mind has been flushed out. The world is so bright and beautiful. I find clarity in this wide-open space.

My thoughts slow down:

Will Josh ever like me?

Why do I like him so much?

Why does Kat call him Joshy?

What about Alex?

Who is he?

Why is this so hard?

Then there are the small voices:

Ohh, that's a good one.

Just one more.

And the big voices:

WHY ARE YOU DOING THIS?

STOP IT!

Now.

I check the clock and it's been thirty minutes, and suddenly the pain bubbles up and the skin on my head is pounding.

I run to the mirror, immediately checking my eyelashes and my head hair and hoping I didn't do anything that can't be hidden. My eyes veer between gray and blue. They are hollow, like the inside of a tunnel that goes on forever.

chapter eight

"Some day my dream is to live on a boat in the middle of the ocean," Alex says, walking beside me as we stroll toward chemistry class. I brush my arm against his as we walk, wondering if he might ever reach out and take my hand.

"Wouldn't that be cool?" he continues. "There would be nothing around except the sea and the sky."

"That sounds lovely," I say, thinking about my ocean daydreams.

"I really do," he says. "It's going to happen some day."

Maybe we can get a boat together, Aurora says. *Just you and me.*

"There's only one problem," he continues. "I can't swim."

"You don't know how to swim?" I stop and turn toward him. "You're joking, right?"

"Shhh," he says, gently pushing my lower back to keep me walking. "I don't want the whole school to know."

"I thought everyone knew how to swim."

"I haven't learned how yet. That's all. I've got time."

"Didn't you get lessons when you were younger?"

"Not everyone is lucky enough to have lessons."

"I can't imagine not knowing how to swim."

Alex shakes his head, looking uncomfortable. "No one ever taught me. Swimming is a luxury, you know."

"Did I ever tell you I used to be on the swim team? I've won ribbons and medals for swimming."

"No," he says. "Although that doesn't surprise me."

"Why didn't you ask for lessons?"

I must look confused because he continues, "Everyone is terrified of sharks because of my mother's death from the attack, even my relatives out here. They think if you get your ankles in water, you might be a goner."

"That's too bad," I say softly. "You aren't scared, though, are you?"

"No way. I'm not scared of anything. Sometimes I imagine what it would be like to be underwater with all the sea creatures and float and watch bubbles under my nose."

Me too, I think. *How weird.*

"Maybe I can show you how sometime," I offer, because I can't help myself.

"Then you'll have to be blindfolded first. I don't want you to see me flailing around in the water."

I don't want you to see me either.

I make a promise to take Alex swimming. I hear the words coming out of my mouth, but I wonder if it's another lie. I would love to show him the peaceful place underwater I know so well.

The next day Alex persists with a text: *When do I get my swimming lesson? You better not forget.*

Soon, I reply. *Don't worry.*

He walks with me to chemistry class all week long. He drops

me off at homeroom too, and sometimes we meet after P.E. By the end of the week, we are lingering. I wish I could slow down time and push the pause button. I could walk all over the world with him and not get bored.

"About that swimming lesson?" he says, bringing it up again.

"Alex, I told you I'll do it." I say, trying to sound reassuring. I think about my hair and how it's harder to hide what is wrong when it's wet.

"We'll have to find a pool with no one around," he says, as if he's reading my thoughts again. "Or maybe we could swim somewhere at night in the darkness. Seriously, I don't want you to see how bad I am."

"Me neither," I say, feeling a pinch in my heart.

He texts me again before the end of the school day: *What are you doing later today? Do you want to come over?*

Come over where? I write, surprised.

My house.

Sure!

We'll have to take the bus.

Sounds good!

I think of Josh and his exclamation points. A little part of me wants to text him and with the news. He's not the only one I like these days.

I make a call to Vivian to let her know I have plans. Not surprisingly, she is busy working and being filmed, but since I haven't been on the schedule for the show this week, she let's me know I am free to do what I want.

"How are you getting to Jasmine's house?" she asks.

"It's not Jasmine, it's Alex," I say. "And we'll be taking the bus."

"The bus?" Vivian asks, like I just told her I'll be riding a UFO.

"You know, the big yellow truck thing with lots of windows."

"Don't be smart with me," she says and I know she doesn't approve. "This isn't the guy from Mexico, is it?"

"Yes, it's him."

"I hope he lives in a safe part of town. I wouldn't want anything terrible happening to you."

"I'm sure it's fine," I moan. "Maybe he's filthy rich. Does it really matter where he's from?"

"So you like him, then?" she asks.

"Kind of. Yes."

"On the Josh Slater level?"

"I don't know," I say. "Maybe."

"Well, have a good time with your boyfriend. I'm seeing mine tonight too."

"He's just a friend…" I start to say, but she has already hung up the phone.

We board the bus and ride together in the back seat, sitting shoulder to shoulder with our knees pressed toward the seat in front of us. I've never ridden the school bus before, but it feels incredibly natural next to Alex.

I try not to think about how our faces are just a few feet apart and how he can see all of my hair perfectly. He is telling me a funny story about his brother and I watch the back of the seat, noticing the indentations. It is strange, but the more we talk, the more comfortable I feel and the more I find myself wanting to face him and gaze into his dark eyes without reservation.

When we get to his house, it's run down like Grandma's place, with peeling grayish blue paint and a lawn that has seen better days.

Alex leads me inside the entryway, telling me to be careful. He explains that crazy Uncle Ringo really isn't his uncle, but he is kind of crazy and a family friend. Alex reminds me that he and his older brother, Marcos, are living here temporarily, since his relatives in San Diego lost their home.

I wonder for a moment if I could ask Vivian to let him stay with us when we move back home. I wonder what she would say. It would be fun to sneak into Alex's room at night. I imagine his arms wrapped around me all night. That would be, pretty much, the best thing ever.

In the hallway magazines are piled everywhere, creating a maze that we can hardly fit through. I fold my arms, stepping through the piles, careful not to bump into anything.

"That's why we call him loco," Alex says, stepping ahead of me and unbuttoning his collared shirt and revealing a t-shirt underneath. "He collects things."

Just like my grandma.

"Couldn't he at least store this stuff in the garage?"

"Can't get in there. It's completely full. The door won't open."

"Wow," I say thinking about the junk museum and how this is actually worse. "This reminds me of my Grandma's house where I'm living now."

"Oh, yeah? I didn't know you were living with your grandma."

"Well, I'm not. She died."

"Oh. I'm sorry."

"I know I should be sad, but I'm not," I continue. "I guess I'm one of those people who just gets over things real fast."

"Sadness is not an obligation," Alex says, meeting my eyes, which suddenly makes me want to cry.

"What was your grandmother like?" he asks. "Did you know her well?"

"No," I say. "We stopped visiting her when I was a kid. It sucks to be living in a stranger's house who was a close relative."

"That's a bummer you never got to know her."

"You're right," I say. "It would have been nice to spend time together before she died"

"I feel the same way about my family. I haven't really known any of them all these years because we've been in different countries. The first chance I have, I'm going back to Mexico, at least for a short time."

"That sounds hard. Do you talk to them often?"

"I talk to my dad sometimes, but things aren't good right now."

"Why?"

"He's dying."

"Oh, I'm so sorry."

"Me too."

I wait for him to say something else, but he doesn't. Instead, he leads me into the kitchen where there are unopened Fanta soda cans stacked on the dining room table.

"Nobody actually drinks that stuff," he says, gesturing toward the Fanta cans. "Uncle Ringo just keeps them around for some reason." Alex grabs us some cold sodas from the fridge.

I wonder if I should ask more about his dad, but I have no idea what else to say. Instead I ask, "Does Uncle Ringo get thirsty a lot?"

"I told you, he collects stuff," Alex says, sliding on a San Diego Padres baseball cap from the coffee table. He turns it around backwards. "He thinks the world is going to end, so he is stocking up on sodas and reading materials, among other things."

I try not to laugh. "So, orange and grape sodas will save us?"

"Didn't you know that? Come on, Alyssa."

Alex leads me into the living room where there are rows and rows of DVDs piled up from floor to ceiling. Above the fireplace mantel are more Fanta soda cans separated and lined up by color.

"He seems a little OCD to me."

"Tell me about it," Alex says. "That's his problem exactly."

"He's really obsessive compulsive?"

"Yeah, I think so. He subscribes to magazine and never reads them, and he buys sodas and never drinks them. The only reason I could invite you over is because he's out of town right now. Otherwise, you would have to go through the basement door and take a shower first. Everything goes through the shower before coming into the house—groceries, the mail, even me and my brother."

"You have to take a *shower* every time you enter your own house?"

"Maybe I shouldn't have invited you here."

"No, no. I'm just surprised. I had no idea there were people out there like that."

"There are all kinds."

Yes, I know.

"I haven't really been truthful with you," I say, holding my breath. "There's something you really should know."

"What do you mean? You don't have anything wrong with you, do you?"

"No, I'm fine," I assure him. I am, right?

"My family is actually filming a reality show right now. That's why we're living at my grandma's house. I've been trying to keep it a secret. And my parents are the ones who have traveled the world, not me. I'm actually from San Diego too."

He is quiet for a moment. "I'm glad you told me."

I explain the show concept and Alex struts over to the pool table and leans over to line up the balls. Part of me wants to just run out of his house and go home because I'm nervous about what I'm doing here.

"Let's play a game," he says, holding up a pool stick.

Normally, the last thing I want to do is play a game I know I suck at, but I agree. Alex sets up the pool table and takes the first shot. When I step up, all my shots seem to go magnetically into the pockets.

"Damn, you're good at this," he says.

"I practice a lot," I lie with a smile.

"This is my worst game ever. You're killing me."

"This is my best ever," I say proudly, shooting the last ball in to win. I have no idea how I do it, but I'll take the win.

"What do you want to do now?" he asks, leaning on the side of the pool table holding the pool stick in his hands.

I want to kiss you now, Aurora says. *Come over here.*

Alex's phone buzzes. "Sorry, I told my brother I'd call him before dinner."

"It's okay. You can get it."

With the phone to his ear, Alex removes the baseball cap, rubbing his hand over his hair. He looks different than he does at school and it makes me like him even more. I love that he doesn't mind me coming over and seeing his house.

Then he puts the baseball cap on my head, even though it goes down past my eyes. I tilt it up. "Keep the hat," he says, turning away from the phone for a second. "You look good in it."

I look out the window, imagining what Aurora would do next. *Tell me more about your dad.*

Alex leaves the room and I sit on the edge of the pool table waiting for him to come back. I am wondering why Alex's dad is dying, but I don't want to make him uncomfortable by asking too much.

When he finally gets off the phone, he tells me that Uncle Ringo is coming home early and his brother will drive me home now.

I try to hide my disappointment, pushing the hat closer to my head.

When I get home I channel surf, trying to find the Home and Garden channel and an old episode of *Kicking it at Grandma's House* (no luck). It's Friday night and I have no plans whatsoever and I wonder what my old friends are doing back home.

I start to write a text to Kat about Alex, and then erase it.

My hands make my way into my hair. I am exploring the crown of my head before I even know what I am doing. After a few minutes I duck into the bathroom and lose track of time. For some reasons these hairs are even more satisfying to pull out than any other—maybe because I can see them easily in the mirror. They feel thicker and more textured.

I don't stop until my phone rings. I see Rachel's name, but don't answer. I feel blank, in another world, transparent.

The phone rings again as I try to snap back into focus. Life is rolling along. Even though time appears to stop in these moments, it's an illusion. The soreness on top of my head suddenly settles in. Damage has definitely been done.

The bathroom floor is littered with strands, more than I've ever seen before. As if moving in slow motion, I scoop the hair into the wastebasket, feeling disgusted like I'm cleaning up a dead rat.

Then I pause at the mirror and to my horror there are two dime-size bald patches at the crown of my head.

HOLY SHIT.

This isn't happening.

They are unmistakable and I part my hair a few different ways, trying to convince myself it's not a big deal. I can cover it up, right?

I sift through the drawers, desperately trying to find a headband or a barrette or something before settling on Alex's baseball cap. Then I pull my hair into a ponytail, but realize there is also missing patch near my ear.

Noooooooooo.

My phone rings again and this time I answer it.

"We're here," Vivian says, sounding breathless.

"Who is here?" I ask, as the front door slams shut downstairs and a bunch of feet march in.

"The film crew," she answers. "We had a change of plans. We need you now."

"This isn't really a good time for me," I say, but she is already gone.

I take a deep breath and say a little prayer.

After all the damage I've just caused, I have to go on camera. I think about Alex and how he is isn't afraid of anything. Then I walk out of the bathroom and slide my hand down the banister and find Vivian sitting on Mighty Mike's lap on the La-Z-Boy.

"There you are," she says, jumping up and handing me a folder. "These are your lines for tonight."

"My lines?" I question, looking at the open page. "I thought this was a reality show."

"Reality Schmality," Mighty Mike says with a laugh. "We need more drama-rama."

I read the script. "Uh, my fondest memory of my grandmother is when we'd make homemade lemonade together and sell it to kids in the neighborhood."

"A little more confidence, Alyssa," the skinny guy says. "Say it like you mean it."

I continue. "Yellow also happens to be my grandmother's favorite color."

Mighty Mike loudly interjects, "But that doesn't mean the color has to stay after grandma's gone. Right?"

"Right," I repeat.

"Right!" Vivian cheers.

"Our team is ready with the newest color in home fashion, phantom blue, to get this house ready for young, hip buyers," Mighty Mike says.

"We cannot wait to see the transformation," Vivian adds. Then she studies me, frowning. "I don't think you should wear that hat. It's much too big for your head."

Just as I am about to protest that big hats are cool, Mighty Mike says, "The hat is good for her character, actually. It gives the impression that the rebellious teenage daughter is ready to do some special work in memory of her grandma. We'll give Alyssa a paint brush and let her do the first stroke in casual wear."

I nod in agreement, like I planned it all along, but I feel sick at the thought of the camera lights focusing on my imperfections. First, I'll need to duck into the bathroom again, adjusting the baseball cap to be perfectly balanced on my head.

"Alyssa, are you ready?" Vivian asks a few minutes later.

"Yes," I say weakly, following her to the front yard. I recite my lines a few more times, trying to sound sincere, although it is hard since the closest Grandma and I got to making lemonade was when she sent me lemon drops in an Easter basket one time.

The camera crew sets up lights on the front lawn and a few curious neighbors gather around to watch. A small crowd has gathered on the sidewalk. A couple of kids have set up a table and a pizza delivery car is pulling up to them.

"Wonderful," I say under my breath. "I'm loving the attention right now."

When the shoot starts, my mouth is dry and I jumble up my lines. The lights are as bright as a car's headlights and I feel them swallowing me whole.

When we are finally done, a little girl sneaks into the yard and approaches me. "Hi," she says, waving to get my attention. She holds out a notepad and a magic marker. "Can I get your autograph?"

I start to laugh. "Me?"

"Yes, you," she says.

I take the cap off the marker and scribble *Aurora Stone*.

"Thanks!" the little girl chimes, running back to the sidewalk.

"Sure thing," I say, trying not to laugh.

When I get back into the house I find Vivian's lips on Mighty Mike's and not just kissing, but making out with tongue action. Mighty Mike has her pushed up against Grandma's bucking bronco lamp in the living room, his hands in her cleavage.

I immediately turn the opposite direction, bumping into a ceramic cat and hoping neither of them saw me.

Then I run upstairs and lock myself in my room, putting a chair in front of the door to keep everyone out. I pick up my phone to call Rachel back.

"Hello?" she answers. "How are you doing?"

I tell her that I'm fine, but my hands are shaking. I am thankful we don't know each other well and she can't detect how upset I am.

"You're not going to believe this, but I just signed an autograph," I say. "This little girl came up to me on the front lawn."

"Wow, that is a riot," Rachel says.

"It is, isn't it?" I say, but my voice is sad.

"Alyssa, are you okay? You don't sound right."

"I'm fine. I've just had it with this stupid show."

"If you ever need someone to talk to, you can always call me. I'm here for you. All right?"

"Thanks," I say, removing the hat and feeling myself fade away. I avoid my reflection in the window.

I know the bald spots are clear as day.

chapter nine

I quickly become the girl who wears ponytails or barrettes to school, the girl with a mirror in her pocket and a makeup bag always handy. I steal false eyelashes from Vivian's cosmetics collection. I practice gluing the lashes on, noticing they look real. I become the girl who masters wearing those lashes to school and even sleeping in them.

I am getting worse and I don't know how to stop.

Every morning I spend an extra two hours trying to hide the habit that is both destroying me and preserving my sanity. I wake up and take a shower before Vivian is out of bed. My barrette goes in the same place on top of my head with a few squirts of hairspray. This becomes my routine.

The weather has gotten cooler and some of the trees are changing colors. I can feel the change in the air and even my texts to Kat have changed. We don't write to each other as often. She is busy with cheerleading and sometimes I wonder how I lived for so long attached to her hip.

"Let's go, girls," Coach Roach, says, clapping her hands and shooing us out to the soccer field like we are cattle.

I'm in P.E. class and have just checked the mirror about a hundred times to make sure I look okay.

I run with the other girls, reminding myself that if I start to sweat I have to remember not to rub my face too much.

Thank god we don't have to use the pool.

I've somehow managed to keep convincing Alex I will take him swimming, while delaying the idea as long as possible. I can see him across the soccer field with the other guys, but I'm not sure if he'd ever noticed me in the blur of gym clothes. He is the only guy wearing red sneakers. You can see them a mile away.

Rachel, Toni, and I make it out to the center of the field and pretend to participate in playing soccer. We do just enough to keep Coach Roach off our backs. Toni has a nail file in her hand and is using it to shoo away a bee, while Rachel does cartwheels and eggs me on to try one.

"I don't have the coordination," I tell her, which isn't true. If I go upside down, who knows what will happen to my barrette.

The ball whirls past us and I feel a little sad I'm not trying harder to participate. I like sports, but it's not worth the risk of exposing my problem.

Coach Roach yells at us and Rachel starts skipping down the field toward the goal post. We're near the other field, where the guys are playing.

"Do you see your guy anywhere?" Rachel asks me.

I blush. I mentioned my interest in Alex to her, making her swear on her deathbed that she wouldn't make a big deal about it.

"Darth Vader, three o'clock," I say, using our code name.

"Which one?" she asks, scanning the guys.

I lower my voice. "He's cute, black hair, red shoes."

"He's looking at us."

"He is not."

"He's looking at *you*."

I don't know how it happens, but the next thing I know something really hard slams into the back of my head and I am horizontal watching the grass. My eyes zero in on the yellow blades on top of each piece. A few thoughts pass like, *I'll just lay here the rest of class. They can play over me. I'll be fine.*

Then the athletic girls are hovering over me and I realize I should get up as one of them says, "She's conscious. Come on, who gets hit in the *back* of the head by the soccer ball?"

"Are you okay?" Rachel asks.

"Wonderful," I answer. "I feel awesome."

Rachel stifles a laugh, covering her mouth. Toni giggles too, tucking her nail file into the waistband of her shorts. I am not going to torture myself by checking out what the guys are doing on the other field. My head aches too much.

I sit up and realize everyone is staring at the place where my bald spots were covered up by a strategically placed barrette. I instinctively reach my hand up to feel for the metal clip. It is gone.

I try not to panic, tossing my hair to one side.

"Everything okay?" Coach Roach inquires, asking to see the bump.

"I'm okay," I say, keeping my head tilted. "Do you see my barrette anywhere?"

Everyone is watching me except for Rachel and Toni, who are scanning the grass.

"Let me see it a little closer," Coach Roach says.

"Actually, I don't feel so good," I say, standing up.

"I need to take a look," Coach Roach insists, coming closer. I know she wouldn't be so curious if I wasn't trying so hard to conceal my head. "I'm sure it's fine, but I need to check."

"No!" I say, feeling frantic. "I need to be excused."

"Are you sure you're okay?"

"Yes, please let me go," I plead.

I turn and run toward the building, hearing Rachel call out my name, but I am too panicked to wait for her. I pull open the heavy door and enter the quiet locker room, going toward the mirror. The fluorescent lights above my head are unflattering enough, but I've avoided looking at myself like this, in daylight, without adjusting anything.

What have I done to myself?

The bald spots are bigger now, marking the top of my head like a red X. I can't believe the amount of hair that is missing, more than I realized. People are going to talk if they haven't started already.

Up until this moment, it hasn't hit me that it is going to be months, maybe years until I can wear it all down again without a barrette. Even then I might have to get a boy haircut.

I can't think of anything worse.

I gather it into a thin ponytail. I want to cry so badly, but I am not about to do a public experiment to see what crying can do to false eyelashes. I quickly grab my stuff out of my locker and call Vivian.

"Is this one of your stomach aches?" she asks, as we drive to the doctor's office.

"Yeah," I say, as I watch the cars go by.

"I know the move has been hard on you, but we had to do it."

I nod as we drive past the Las Vegas strip on the freeway, the billboards and casino lights blinking and bright just the way they are at midnight. I feel like a baby, like I am acting weak when I am supposed to be strong.

Unbreakable. Isn't that the way we're supposed to be?

"Sorry I've left you home alone so much," Vivian says.

I shrug. I'm still mad at Vivian for letting Mighty Mike feel her up in the living room. He seems like such a predator now.

"Sometimes you have to go with the flow," Vivian says.

"Right."

I don't feel like listening to her. Instead, I turn my head toward the red mountains in the distance. They remind me of painted Hollywood scenery. I have this familiar sense that I am in a movie and none of this is real.

An hour later I am lying on a table with Dr. Blahner hovering over me with her fish-like hands.

"Just call me Dr. Blah," she says, like this is a great joke.

My back is pressed against the table and I gaze at the black dots on the ceiling panels as Dr. Blah examines me. I count to twenty, feeling myself relax. This weird part of me likes being poked and prodded, like I am a puzzle that someone else can solve. All I have to do is lie still and stare out into space, hoping the pieces fit together.

Dr. Blah turns to Vivian. "Is your daughter having any other problems?"

"Just these stomach aches," Vivian says. She has been having them for years. It seems like she has a lot of mysterious health problems."

I swallow hard, hoping she won't ask too many questions.

"Is there anything else?" Dr. Blah asks, looking from me to Vivian.

"Oh wait, her shoulder," Vivian says. "She pulled a muscle while swimming a few months ago."

Dr. Blah feels my shoulder, rotating my arm and giving me a funny look. "We should do some tests," she says, thumbing through some paperwork and whipping a pen out of her pocket.

I immediately sit up and protest. "No tests needed."

"What do you mean?"

"I think it's just my nerves."

I turn to Vivian, noticing the clumps of mascara at the ends of her lashes and I freeze, like I am waiting for her to tell the doctor that mine are missing.

"I know she has had a hard time adjusting to the move," Vivian says on cue.

I nod in agreement, but then Vivian says, "If this keeps happening, we will need more tests."

I don't like the idea of tests, so I sit up a little straighter, like I'm feeling better now.

"Are you feeling anxious?" Dr. Blahner asks.

Anxious, I ask myself. *Sure, why not?*

Worried? Yes, a little.

I wonder if I should ask her about getting vaccinated.

"Heart racing? Feeling overwhelmed? Panicky?" Dr. Blahner continues.

"Uh huh," I say, noticing that she likes these answers.

"I think there is something that might help you."

Everyone conveniently forgets about the soccer ball incident and I make up a story to Coach Roach about having killer cramps. My hair is now in a ponytail, with a headband around my head.

Attractive.

Every day now I wear it in a ponytail, wondering if this is how it'll be the rest of my life. Other girls style their hair up every day, right? I search for them like we are in this club together. Mostly, I see girls who have baggy clothes, no makeup, and look more like boys. I wonder what they are hiding.

The only person who shows concern in P.E. class is Rachel. I am lingering in the bathroom stall with my compact mirror and makeup bag held tightly in the palm of my hand. I've been waiting for everyone to leave and apparently she is doing the same.

"What happened the other day?" she asks, following me as I leave the stall and go back toward the lockers.

I turn, dropping the mirror and makeup into my gym locker. "My stomach hurt so I went to the doctor," I answer.

I sit on the bench and tie my shoelaces, noticing Rachel's silence. "I hate this class," I say, trying to change the subject. "Do you think Coach Roach would notice if we just sat in here?"

She ignores me. "Getting hit in the head gave you a stomach ache? That doesn't make sense."

I can tell she is genuinely concerned. Her eyes seem to say that it is okay.

"I was already feeling sick, so it just made it worse."

"Why didn't you wait for me? I was running after you."

"I told you I was sick."

"I came into the locker room and you were gone. I was worried about you."

I shake my head, standing up to head outside. "I'm sorry. I didn't feel good."

"Wait," Rachel says. "Can I ask you something else?"

I'm afraid to turn around and hear her question. I am already thinking up numerous lies, cuing them up in my mind. Depending on what she asks I can have a clever answer ready.

"I'm having a sleepover next weekend. Do you want to come?"

The question is so ordinary it startles me. "Sure. I'd love to."

"Great. I'll let you know the time and everything later."

Rachel and I walk outside together and there is this weird silence between us. It's the kind of silence that friends shouldn't have. Even though I haven't known Rachel long, it already feels there is a wall forming.

I know this is the turning point I have been waiting for, the sign that this is a real problem and I need help.

I have a prescription for an antidepressant in my bag.

Dr. Blahner thinks this will help me adjust to the change and anxiety of the move. I don't want to take drugs, especially since I know Vivian is a fan and kids at school say they make you feel numb.

Later I will drop the prescription off in the pharmacy and carry out my pills, but instead of taking one, I leave them in the bag, unsettled by the idea.

"Once you start taking these pills, you never go back," Vivian warned. "Look at me. I'm happy with myself. I thank my medicine cabinet every morning."

Something about her warning makes me want to get better my way.

I vow to stop NOW.

To start, I steal more stuff from Vivian's beauty collection, including gloves to wear over my hands and a relaxation CD. I find another forum online and post my declaration to end this ridiculous problem. I am done being this way.

Four days later I take out a calendar before bed and put three stickers on it, indicating that I've been good. I know I can do this cold turkey.

Plenty of times I've stopped myself, or had no desire to pull. But I've never tried when it's all I want to do. Instead, I pick the bumps on my legs and arms, bite the skin around my nails, and nearly pull out a handful of hair. The reddish-brown strands are held tightly between my fingertips like I've finally found some air.

Volts of electricity are running down my body. Relaxing is impossible. It's time for bed and I'm awake, filled with energy, like my nerve endings are on the outside of my skin and lit up. I pick out an outfit for school and then without even thinking about what I'm doing I bring my hand to my eye, whipping out a few new lashes.

I swallow, feeling the shame trickle down my throat. In one second I have caused weeks worth of damage.

Somehow I finally make it into bed, sipping some warm tea and turning the lamp off to hide the coral color of the bedroom walls. I put socks over my hands, securing them with hair ties on my wrists. Then I close my eyes.

Aurora Stone is with Hoffman again and they are walking through the fields at night. They are beneath a full moon, heading toward a creek, hand in hand, passing through the tall grass.

"Wait," Aurora calls, as Hoffman drops her hand and darts forward. "Where are you going?"

"I want to show you something," he says, leading her to a grove of trees near a creek.

For some reason under these trees there are fireflies everywhere. They glow in the night, circling the tree and landing in the palm of Hoffman's hand.

"Check this out," he says, releasing one of the fireflies into the air, revealing a beautiful tree house above them, complete with a roof and multiple levels. There is a ladder leading up to it and Aurora starts to climb it.

I let go of the image for a moment, feeling each follicle alive and pulsating under my skin. There is a gnawing inside, a sense of urgency. This is the most I have ever tried to resist the urge. The strongest I have said no.

I try to go back into the scene with Aurora and Hoffman, but instead, in that foggy area between sleep and awake, I am standing near the grove of trees, but they appear very different.

Instead, there is just one giant tree in a fog—I cannot even find the top when I look up. I am like a tiny microbe, witnessing it in awe.

And then I realize it's not really a tree. It's a hair. The biggest one I have ever seen.

I reach out for it, mesmerized, and then just as I am about to touch it, everything goes dark. This is the hair that would surpass all others.

The perfect pull.

chapter ten

Over the next few weeks the crew of *Kicking it at Grandma's House* works around the clock. Grandma's barnyard kitchen is transformed into a sterile, modern square of space with oversized, metallic appliances and sharp edges. The next stage is the basement, then the bedrooms, followed by the living room and a big finish with the landscaping

One morning I wake up extra early, remembering that a set of index cards I need is downstairs on the coffee table. The house is quiet as I open my bedroom door, tiptoeing out into the hallway.

My hair hangs below my shoulders, thinned out with the obvious bald patches at the top that I haven't bothered covering.

In the living room, heavy brown drapes hang from floor to ceiling and I part the drapes to look out the window. Just as I let the morning light fill part of the room, Vivian's head pops up from the couch.

I gasp, turning to face her. "You scared me. What are you doing out here?"

"Sleeping," she answers, even though she is dressed and ready for work, with just a light blanket on top of her. "Mighty Mike and I were in the casino all night. What are you doing?"

"Looking for my index cards," I say, feeling the sunlight on my back.

I try to think of something else to say, realizing that the top of my head is entirely exposed.

"I haven't seen them," Vivian says, and in that moment I know, *she knows*.

"They must be here somewhere," she says, sitting up and pressing her hands between the couch cushions.

"Yeah," I say, realizing I feel incredibly calm.

Amazingly, it's a wave of relief. I am struck by the feeling of my feet on the floor, solid and steady. I imagine the rocks and soil packed below us, holding everything up, including me.

I move closer to Vivian, letting her see the real me in the light of the morning. "I don't think the cards are here," I say. "They must be in my locker at school."

Vivian nods, glancing at me sheepishly and yawning. Then she marches to the kitchen for her usual cup of coffee. "I think I'm hung over. Might as well start the day on an early note."

I follow her. "I guess you know now."

"Know what?"

"Well, look at me," I say.

Vivian stops, her blue icicle eyes on mine. "What happened to your hair?"

"I have this problem…" I start to say.

"Are you pulling it out?" she asks, point blank.

"How did you know?"

"I'm your mother. I'm supposed to be intuitive."

"Are there hidden cameras in the bathroom?" I ask.

"No."

I swallow, not sure if I believe her. My skin feels prickly at the thought of someone watching me. "Then how do you know?"

"I've seen a lot of hair in the trash, Lissy. I wanted to say something earlier, but I didn't know how to bring it up. We can get you different pills or a wig or some extensions."

I nod, letting it sink in that she knows. And she's *okay*.

"You haven't told anyone else, have you?" she asks, hesitating and taking two new coffee mugs out of the cupboard. "People are not going to understand if you announce this to the whole world, or walk around in public like that. Have you told Frankie or anyone with the show?"

"No one," I whisper.

"Have you told your father?"

I let out a laugh. "Why would I tell him? We never talk."

"You might. I don't know when you talk to him."

"Did you tell him about you and Mighty Mike?"

"I did not," she says, fiddling with the coffee pot. "I would keep this—all of this—between you and me. You wouldn't want your friends at home to know, right?"

I shake my head, thinking that it doesn't matter much anymore since my friends at home are more like strangers now. I hardly knew what to say to Kat with her cheerleading stories and such. Her texts no longer amuse me.

#23 Gabe. Remember him? Graduated last year.

Be careful with the older guys, okay?

Are you still at #0?

Of course.

Josh would kiss you if you were here.

Stop saying stuff like that.

I'm serious!

"We'll need to keep this from the camera crew," Vivian continues, her mind churning. "You don't want to put yourself in front of a firing squad."

"You're right," I say, thinking how one bad moment can spread like wildfire. "I don't want anyone to know. I'm sure I can keep a low profile. Maybe I'll get better soon."

"Good," she says. "I'll do whatever I can to help you."

I ride the bus with Alex again, this time wearing a headband around the top of my head and anticipating the hair extensions Vivian says we can get from a stylist. I hope it works.

"I want to show you something," he says.

We get off at a different stop than before, in a different neighborhood, and walk for a few blocks and then head down a dirt trail next to a long cement wall. This is a neighborhood I have never been to before. The houses are larger and spaced farther apart, many with long gated driveways.

"Is this a short cut or something?" I ask, adjusting my bag. The adobe roof tiles and private entrances remind me of home, minus the dry desert air.

"Follow me," Alex says.

Eventually we reach a gated area, along the back side of a property.

Alex dials a code to unlock the gate.

"Do you know who lives here?"

"Kind of," he says, pushing open the gate and holding up some overgrown tree branches for me to step under.

"Aren't we trespassing?" I ask, going through the gate with hesitation.

"Depends how you look at it," he says. "Just trust me."

We step through an area filled with broken tree branches and overgrown grass into the top of a back yard.

I stop abruptly and realize we've arrived at one of the largest mansions in Las Vegas. It faces a hillside and resembles a medieval castle. The grassy yard is enormous and lined with palm trees and intricate gothic statues.

"What do you think?" Alex asks.

"This is amazing," I say, although I have to admit the lush landscaping isn't that different from my own yard back home. There is an area that resembles a jungle that leads into an oval-shaped swimming pool with a stone mermaid on top of a rock waterfall looking over it. It's tucked deep into the backyard with boulders and a small fence surrounding it. The water is an inviting turquoise color.

"I thought you'd like this," Alex says, smiling.

"How did you know the code to get in here?"

"I worked here over the summer doing landscaping. See those bushes over there?" he asks, pointing to a row above a dragon figure. "I trimmed them. Those roses? I planted them. Even those stone steps next to the pool. I helped place each one with my hands."

I take a deep breath, admiring the scenery. I've never thought much about the people who build things, who set foundations and create places out of dust.

"Those trees we walked through were cut by my brother, Marcos," he continues, shifting his weight in the mess of tree branches. "He always did a sloppy job, but nobody ever came up here."

"I see."

"Yeah, I kind of miss this place," Alex says. "I always meant to sneak into the pool area."

"Are you thinking what I'm thinking?" I ask, ignoring the alarms in my head.

Alex grins, but shakes his head sadly.

"We could come back at night," I suggest.

"Believe me, I'd love to, but I can't."

"Why? Because you can't swim? That is not an excuse. Think about how much you helped build this place. Maybe we could even ask the owner for his permission."

Alex laughed. "That won't happen."

"It's just a thought. I mean, it is a private pool and you need to learn to swim."

"The owner wouldn't know me from a guy on the street," Alex says. "We were just some kids hired to do landscaping. Nobodies."

"Did you ever talk to him?"

"Yes, and he spoke to us only in Spanish. I don't know if he realized we speak English."

"I'm surprised you wouldn't have corrected him."

"Sometimes you play along. You give people what they expect so they don't ask questions. It's easier that way."

"I know what you mean."

I glance at the arch-shaped windows on the second story of the mansion, thinking about my house back home and wondering how something so beautiful could also be so sad.

chapter eleven

On the night of Rachel's sleepover I am super nervous and decide to stay for just a few hours, rather than the whole night. I feel bad about it, but there is no good way to predict what bald spots might become exposed with my head against a pillow. I wear my headband covering the top of my head now and the rest of my hair in the usual curly ponytail.

Even with the bald spots and amount of time spent pulling, it's amazing how much hair I still have, but it's disappearing fast.

"I wish you could stay the whole night," Rachel says, escorting me inside. Immediately, I wish I lived in her house. There is a montage of family photos lining the wall against a staircase and a few area rugs. The place is totally welcoming like a warm hug.

Toni and two other girls are in the kitchen making popcorn on the stovetop. "I got a bunch of foreign films and Toni wants to watch a Marilyn Monroe movie she found in her parents collection. You can stay at least until midnight, right?"

"Yes, that's when my ride will be back," I say. Vivian agreed that with my hair situation, she would pick me up.

Everything is so normal at Rachel's house I'm envious. She has a little sister and older brother and there is artwork plastered on the fridge. Her parents are busy making veggie burgers on the grill outside. They have a wild family dog who is running loops around the living room furniture, making her little sister screech with laughter.

"Sorry it's chaotic in here," Rachel says, apologizing for the dog, who barks playfully at me, but I really like it. It feels like the way a house should be, like when you look into a window and there is the definition of a family.

I think of my house back home in San Diego, so large and quiet. I don't want to go back there.

"I wish I could stay longer tonight," I say. "It's nice here."

"You should!" Rachel says. "We have extra pillows and sleeping bags."

I look down at my hands, wanting so much to tell her the truth. "I really shouldn't with the show and everything. They always want to do more filming. It's exhausting."

We chat some more and move the living room furniture so there is room for everyone on the floor in front of a giant flat screen. Rachel goes ahead and rolls out a sleeping bag for me and I lay down with everyone in front of the TV after dinner.

By the middle of the second movie, it's 12:15 and I text Vivian.

Sorry Lissy, she writes. *Can I pick up you in the morning instead? At the casino and drunk as a skunk.*

Somehow this doesn't surprise me and yet it is infuriating. I shift around on the floor and punch in a text back to her that I will delete. I am furious and wonder why I even bother trusting her.

"Everything okay?" Rachel asks, sensing my anger.

105

"No," I say, getting up. "I just need to go outside for a moment. I'll be right back."

I make my way to the front door. I sort of want to do something unexpected like run away. I imagine myself walking down Rachel's driveway and out into the street and hitchhiking out of the city. I could get a waitressing job at a diner somewhere and change my name and hopefully start looking older. It's not that hard to disguise yourself and disappear.

Maybe I could even go to a police station and turn myself in and ask for different parents. Wasn't there a kid who did that one time? Except the police would think I'm insane because I live in a big house by the ocean. It's like sometimes I wish something big was wrong so I would have a reason.

"Alyssa?" Rachel says softly, opening the door behind me. "You can stay the night if you need to, or my mom said she could drive you home. Although it is getting late."

"I don't want to go home."

"Is everything okay?"

"It's okay, but not the best. I really do want to stay."

Rachel folds her arms and she looks cold, even though it's warm outside. "I'm your friend no matter what," she says. "I know we don't know each other that well, but I really like you and if you need to you can tell me anything."

"Thanks," I say, looking down. "Do you have a toothbrush I can borrow?"

"Sure, let's go back inside and I'll get you one."

I take a deep breath and compose a simple text to Vivian to let her know everything is fine and I am staying over at Rachel's. Then I put my phone away. I won't hear back from her.

Rachel takes me into the bathroom and returns with some pajama bottoms with bunnies on them and a t-shirt. I get changed and tighten my ponytail and we brush our teeth at the same time and I see myself in the mirror next to her. Her hair is pulled out of her face and she looks pretty without a trace of makeup.

I also see a pair of tweezers on the countertop, innocently placed.

"I need to tell you something," I say.

Rachel promises she can keep a secret and I close the bathroom door.

"I have to keep this on all the time," I say, referring to the bandana. I touch the rubber band on my ponytail "And this pulled back too." I'm not about to remove anything on my head.

"Do whatever you need to do. I'm not judging you."

"Thanks." I shrug my shoulders. "I have to wear my eye makeup to bed also. My head hair is thinning, too. It's really awful. I think I have this weird hair-pulling disorder."

"Is there anything I can do to help?"

"I don't know. It just keeps getting worse."

I feel a lump in my throat. "I think I might need to start wearing a wig so my hair might change a little. Like, it might be straighter or something. I don't know if they make curly wigs."

"I'm sure they do. I'm also sure you can get better. You seem like such a strong person."

"I hope so. I guess the main thing is, you'll still be my friend, right? And if you see a bald spot, you won't disappear?"

"I like hanging out with you. I don't care about your hair. Maybe you can get extensions or something. The headband works great. Is this why you ran away from P.E. that one day?"

I nod. "I'm getting some extensions next week. Hopefully they will make it look better."

"They will. I'm glad you told me. We all have problems, you know?" Rachel wipes her hands on one of the towels and I can see the pain in her eyes. "Are you coming back downstairs or what?"

"Yes."

When Vivian drives me to my hair appointment the next week, she grills me about the pulling. Sometimes it is hard to predict what her concern of the day is going to be, but today it is clear that it's all about me.

How much hair is missing?

Why are you doing it more often?

Do you want to start wearing a wig?

My answers are short because the truth is that I don't know why I am doing it and if I could stop, I would. I would have never started. I don't think she believes me.

Plus, I'm still mad at her for leaving me at Rachel's. What if I hadn't been able to spend the night? What if I had to take a taxi home? Would that even be safe? I don't dare bring it up, but it infuriates me.

"You better start changing your game," she warns, inhaling a cigarette and blowing smoke out the window. "I don't want to have a daughter who looks like a freak show. I know you don't want that either."

"I'm trying, okay?"

"Good. Because I don't think your friends back home will be as forgiving. You still want to have friends, right? Any little flaw and those girls could turn their backs on you. Even Kat."

I know Vivian is trying to be helpful and motivate me, but it's having the opposite effect. Because the truth is that she's probably right.

When I meet Jodee, the hair stylist at the salon, I turn into a mechanical person, facing the enemy. Hair on the floor. Hair in magazines. Hair everywhere.

I want to point it out to her like a kid in a museum.

Now that Vivian and Rachel know something is wrong and that I'm going to get better somehow, I've given myself this weird sense of permission to do it more, which of course I keep very quiet. I figure I might as well get it all out of my system. I have gone from barrettes to headbands to daily ponytails to wondering how I'm going to set foot outside the bathroom door.

I imagine Jodee must know something since Vivian chose her as my stylist, but as I sit in her salon chair and she takes out my barrettes and bandana, she is looking at all the patches in wonderment.

"What would you like today?" she asks.

My face reddens and I look at my reflection. I feel like a monster.

"Um, how about some layers and hair extensions?"

I hate the thought of layering my hair but it makes sense to try to cover the bald spots, which are multiplying by the day.

Jodee combs her fingers through my hair. "Do you want to stay a brunette?"

"Yes," I say, wanting to keep my hair as much the same as possible.

"We can do red highlights and add some extensions," she

says, "but if these patches keep expanding, it's going to be very uneven. You might want to change shampoos or try a moisturizing conditioner."

"Will do," I say, trying to sound stoic. "It has been falling out ever since we moved here. The air is so dry here."

"Falling out?" she asks, touching the spots as if they might bite her. "Are you sure?"

"Yeah," I say, wanting to dismiss the subject. "Maybe you could just shave my head or something."

Jodee's big grin fades. "I'll go get the extensions."

I sit back in the chair, suddenly aware of eyes on me. The salon patrons are walking past, no doubt wondering what kind of problem I have, or what kind of stylist could have messed me up this bad. I bite my lip and stare at my hands, trying not to get upset.

I think about leaping out of my chair, but I know I *need* this haircut.

When Jodee comes back, I can hardly look at her and manage to get out a squeak to ask if there is any way we could go somewhere in the salon that is less prominent.

"Sure," she says, leading me into a back windowless room. I wonder if she is ashamed to be working on someone like me.

My hair gets washed and trimmed and Jodee works quietly while I shut my eyes and pretend I am somewhere under the ocean being swept away in a current.

When I open my eyes, my hair is parted in on the opposite side and looks thicker, yet the slightest gust of wind will tell you something is wrong. I am handed some dusty brochures about alopecia and even one about trichotillomania and reading material about hair growing pills and stuff.

I shove the samples and brochures into my bag. I'll never come in here again.

During the car ride home I avoid Vivian's questions about the makeover and if I want to be filmed this evening for the show. I realize I don't want to do anything except crawl into my bed and fall asleep for a long time.

"Did you hear about my procedure next week?" she asks, as we enter the house, which smells like wet paint. A few of the workers from the reality show walk by us and nod.

"What procedure?" I ask, already dreading the answer.

"New boobies," she explains with a robot smile that matches her icicle eyes. "Dr. Young thinks they are too big and I agree. I'm getting them replaced with a new technology that will make them look totally natural, while keeping me in perfect Barbie proportions. Otherwise, your hot momma is going to lose her famous nickname."

No more Barbie Lady. Would that be so tragic?

"It's gonna be a big day for me," she says. "They are going to film the procedure for the show. I would appreciate your support."

"Supported," I say dryly.

"This is big stuff, Lissy" she continues. "But it seems like every time I tell you about good things happening in my life you have this nasty look on your face. I know we don't care about the same things, but that scowl is going to make you need Botox before you graduate from college. You know that, right?"

I can't answer, because if I do I will start screaming. And then I'm not sure what will happen next

Instead, I notice the sounds of the traffic and dogs barking and how the air here is so dry it makes the inside of your nose itch.

Vivian finally stops speaking.

I head straight up the stairs into my room with the awful red walls and twist the blinds shut. I turn my phone ringer off and bury myself under the covers of this bed that doesn't belong to me.

I am exhausted, yet I can't fall asleep. I wonder if there are any sleeping pills somewhere in this house I could take. The effort to actually get up and look for them is too much right now.

Instead, I close my eyes and curl up to my imagination.

Aurora climbs the ladder into the tree house with Hoffman right behind, and when they get to the top, he slips his arms around her. The dark field stands before them in every direction with crickets chirping loudly and the night deepens.

"Hi," he whispers, kissing her softly.

"Hi," she says, breathing in the kiss.

"Did you know that fireflies glow to attract mates?"

"I didn't," she says, leaning over the ledge to gaze down. "That's so amazing."

"Just like you." Hoffman says, taking her hands in his. "I love you."

"I love you too." Aurora feels her body warm with delight.

Everything is frozen in this one blissful moment. The stars and moonlight shine in the field with the fireflies doing their beautiful mating dance. It is as if the earth is fastened together by steel cables locked into one position.

Hoffman falls asleep on the tree house floor with Aurora in his arms, but she stays awake, watching the shadows of the tree branches around them. The sound of crickets becomes softer, a reminder of everything shifting.

Somewhere it is daylight. Somewhere people are in traffic. Somewhere deep under the ocean invisible creatures are alive in a black dust.

Aurora thinks of the porch swing where she and Hoffman spent the summer. It is leaning against the house now, broken apart in two pieces. It is impossible for perfect things to stay the same forever.

We are all like that, she thinks. *Breaking and growing older and wondering what will happen.*

I finally fall asleep and don't wake up until morning.

chapter twelve

It's almost noon and I'm still in bed. I see I've missed a few texts from Kat. She is looking for me, wanting to talk.

I'm here, I write.

Got news. You might not like it.

What is it? I ask, sitting up and remembering the bald spots on my head. My stomach sinks.

Homecoming dance coming up this weekend.

Are you going?

Yeah. Josh asked me to go.

Don't you have other options?

He was the first one to ask.

That doesn't sound like a good idea.

I know. But I felt bad turning him down.

So you're taking pity on him?

We're just going as friends.

Fine. Doesn't bother me. Do what you want.

But you like him. Right?

Liked. Past tense.

He would have asked you if you were here.

Well I'm not there. So don't worry about it.

You sure?

Oh my god. Can we please stop having this conversation?

I can already envision the upcoming text with Josh's name and # sign, indicating a kiss. I want to tell Kat that, like Vivian, she can do what she wants because I don't care anymore. I'll be asleep and dreaming, waiting for it all to get better.

And then Kat writes something that I can't ignore.

By the way, I heard about your mom.

What did you hear?

Jill has been reading her blog. We're excited about the big day tomorrow!

I know Vivian writes about her upcoming surgeries, but I didn't think any of my friends ever read that thing. I search for Vivian's site and click on it.

The home page is pink and black and decorated with the image of a blonde Barbie doll, highlighting that Vivian's proportions are similar, with arrows pointing to different areas of the body.

I see photo after photo of Vivian, showing her progress over the years up until today. You can see the lines around her eyes fade away, her face begin to have this doll-like appearance, and the oddness of her exact proportions. I realize her many surgeries have made her fascinating. It's so different from real life where you can detect the slightest imperfection in her eyes or smile.

No wonder she has thousands of fans.

I set out to look like a real life doll, she writes. *I hope to prove that this is possible. Other people have tried, but I am here to say the Barbie Lady is here to stay! My latest procedure will be detailed on a top-secret*

115

reality show that I will disclose to readers when filming is over. Thanks for all the support, fellow Barbies and wannabes!

As I read the last line, it occurs to me that Vivian doesn't ever mention that she has a daughter, or my father, or anything about our lives. You wouldn't know that she has anything else important.

I insert an anonymous comment: *Hope this surgery is your LAST.*

The weekend goes by and Josh texts me a few lines that sound like an apology for taking Kat to the dance and explaining that he wished he could have taken me instead. Insert multiple exclamation points.

I write him back, making myself sound busy and happy and normal. Which is pretty much the opposite of how I feel.

Vivian is passed out on painkillers on the living room sofa, the cameras from the show getting a few last clips of her post-surgery before wrapping it up for the day.

I've been asked to stay out of filming, except for some filler shots of me helping the crew paint the basement Sierra White, Vivian's favorite shade, which isn't really a color. It's more of a way to paint a wall and turn it into nothing.

I have paint splattered up to my chin and a bandana over my head, which is the ideal accessory, especially considering that the hair extensions aren't working that great. They cover up the hair near the patches. But I keep pulling whenever I am alone, making the bald spots bigger and bigger.

I take a rest from painting and grab a soda. My phone indicates I have another text from Kat. Instead of replying, I help Frankie sort through Grandma's flag collection in the garage. Then I finish up some laundry and carefully fold my underwear into piles, checking the tags on each one. They've been made all over the world: Taiwan, Maldives, Hong Kong, Israel.

These places I find mysterious and faraway. I feel nearly as far away from Kat right now.

By evening, I decide to call her, feeling guilty. Something could be wrong and here I am comparing my underwear tags for fun.

I close my bedroom door, flopping back on the bed and putting my dirty feet up against the wall.

"Hey," she says, out of breath. "Why didn't you just answer my text?"

"We haven't talked in so long," I say. "I thought it would be nice to call."

"Okay," she says hesitantly. "Well, it's good to hear from you."

"You too," I say, although I immediately wish I would have just texted her. Talking seems too intimate, too much of something that has drained out of our friendship lately.

"So," she says. "What have you been doing?"

"Just stuff," I say, trying to sound like it's been busy. "Painting the house with the film crew and trying to stay out of the way with the reality show."

"Oh yeah, how's that going?"

"Great. Vivian loves it. She is getting her fill of attention every day."

"She is going to be so famous. Not to mention you."

"I hope not."

"Come on, Alyssa, who gets an opportunity like this? You're the only person I know who is so lucky, and yet so ungrateful."

Her comment takes me aback. "This is not something I wanted to do. I would rather be in San Diego right now."

"I just think you should take advantage of it. Make a name for yourself. At least enjoy your fifteen seconds of fame."

"Maybe," I say, my heart sinking.

"That's what I would do, but I know we're nothing alike."

I hear a few bangs on the other end of the phone. "Hey, I'm heading into the garage," she says. "Hold on."

Whenever Kat talks on the phone in the garage it means the conversation is top secret. I imagine her making her way to her dad's tool bench, his surfboards hanging above on the wall.

"How's that guy?" she asks, changing the subject. "His name is Alex, right?"

"He's fine," I say, his name sounding foreign coming from her voice. I already know what's coming, so she might was well say it.

"That's cool," she says. "I hope he asks you out."

"I don't know if he likes me that way," I say, even though I'm pretty sure Alex is attracted to me.

"Do you remember when you'd sleep over at my house in elementary school and we'd play that game?"

"The love stare?"

"Oh yeah, that's the one," she says.

"We'd stare in the mirror and make kissy faces." I smile at the memory. "I think it all started after you kissed the mirror with Vivian's lipstick."

"Then we'd make eyes at the boys on the playground just to see who would look back at us and fall in love," she says nearly finishing my sentence. "We had so much fun back then."

"Yeah," I say, softly. "You know, you could have given me the news in the usual way. I've been waiting to see Josh's name appear on your kissing list."

"We didn't kiss, Alyssa. That's not why I texted you."

I pull the phone away from my ear, and press it back quickly, wondering if I heard her right.

"What happened at the dance?"

"Not much. Afterward, Steve Nolin had a party at his house, which is kind of funny now that I think about it. We ended up playing some dumb drinking game and nobody wanted to drive home. So we camped out in Steve's backyard. He has this adult tree house, where you can climb up and see all the way to the ocean."

The air in my nose is suddenly cold. "A *tree* house?"

"Well, yeah, like a tree house for adults. Kids too, I guess."

"And you went up in it?" I ask, unable to let go of this detail.

"Yes. With Josh and Shannon and a few other people."

"What did it look like?"

"I don't know. It was dark, so I couldn't see everything, but there was a little roof and this platform thing and it was actually really cool. The problem was I was afraid to climb down. So, Josh was nice enough to stay up there with me, and we ended up falling asleep."

"You and Josh… fell asleep… in a tree house?"

"We did," she says. "Why are you so surprised?"

"It's just weird, that's all."

"Honestly, we were kind of drunk and not thinking about what we were doing and how it might affect you."

"Well, you were just sleeping, right?"

"There was a bed up there and some other stuff happened."

I try to breathe, but I am choking on the air and the room is starting to turn upside down.

119

"We were not planning on doing anything and I would have never wanted to hurt you this way," Kat continues, taking a breath. "But it just happened. Josh isn't even my type. He's kind of a nerd boy."

This is so unbelievable that I don't know what to say, and this sound comes out of my throat that sounds like laughing.

"What's so funny?" she asks. "I've been really stressed out to tell you. Holy shit."

I let out another sound that is a combination of a laugh and a wail. I don't know if I'm about to laugh or cry or yelll. I'm having trouble breathing and it feels like someone just sat on my chest and won't get up.

"It's fine," I finally let out, even though I'm not.

"I think I like sex," Kat gushes. "It's kind of addicting."

I don't want to hear *anything* else.

"I'm sorry, Alyssa. I shouldn't have picked him."

"Don't worry. It's not a big deal. You're the one putting yourself at risk for diseases and babies and stuff. I'm not going to the abortion clinic with you."

"Come on. We're not that stupid."

I laugh again, keeping myself from giving her the pleasure of showing I'm upset. "I don't care what you do with him. Did you think I was going to start crying or something?"

"I thought it might bother you."

"I don't care," I repeat. "We both know he liked you all along. Why fight with the obvious?"

"Me? No way. Not Josh. He *always* liked you, but you were too shy with him."

"Not true," I say, shaking my head. "Did he tell you that?"

"Not in those exact words, but you kind of had your chance."

I did?!?

And then I realize she is right.

I stare at the digital clock on the dresser, noting the time of this moment and wanting to push fast forward. It feels like a part of me has just died.

Then I run into the bathroom. This time instead of grabbing the tweezers, I step in front of the toilet. I feel myself gagging, but nothing comes out.

I force myself to believe that everything is fine, that nothing has changed, that my daydreams are just a coincidence, that Kat is still my best friend and Aurora is still imaginary and Josh is still mine. Except I feel betrayed by all of them.

chapter thirteen

"Alyssa Simone, wake up," a male voice calls out.

I turn my head from my pillow, groggy, my eyes opening.

"We need to start filming the bedroom transformations," Mighty Mike says, standing above me. He is wearing his usual tool belt, scruffy overalls, and his dazzling camera-ready hair is styled. "I wanted to give you a moment to get ready."

I reach for the bandana I wore while painting, tying it around my head. I'm tired of these surprises first thing in the morning. A few days have passed since I spoke to Kat, and what's left of my hair is a wreck.

Then the camera lights flicker on. "Good morning from Grandma's house," Mighty Mike says with his boisterous camera voice. "Today we're going to be putting a hole right here in this wall."

He explains to the camera, as it follows him around the room, that the adjacent bedroom is being used as a storage area and that a larger bedroom suite would add value to the home. Then he knocks his fist against the wall near the foot of my bed.

"BA-BYE Mr. Wall."

The door next to my room has been kept locked all this time. I honestly thought it was another closet.

"How do you feel about the transformation Alyssa?" he asks.

"Amazing," I say, reading the cue card behind him without a hint of expression. "Couldn't be any more excited."

"Then I have another surprise for you," he says. "Step back."

I wonder what he means, and then hear a terrible grinding noise that gets louder. A chainsaw from the opposite bedroom penetrates through the wall, cutting open a large circle and sending a cloud of dust into my room.

I start coughing and catch my breath.

"You're taking my wall down RIGHT NOW!?"

I leap off the bed, aware that I'm still in my army print boxer shorts and a t-shirt with a green Oompa Loopa on the front.

"Pretty soon," Mighty Mike says, peeking through the hole, where a camera waits on the other side. "Nice job, Frankie."

Even though I've been trying to behave, we've reached my threshold. I hadn't realized anyone was going to wake me up and barge into my room, let alone *open a hole in the wall.* I don't understand why it has to be my room that needs this first thing in the morning.

Apparently the "fun" part of the show is continuing to live in the house while it basically gets demolished.

I burst past Mighty Mike and out into the hallway where Vivian is standing in matching baby blue sweat pants and sweatshirt, looking innocent.

"Did you know they were going to do this today?" I demand.

"Lissy, we needed an authentic reaction from you. The show

isn't going to be believable if we are always reciting lines all the time."

"Are they seriously going to knock down my wall right now?"

"Sorry, but I think it's all true. Mighty Mike is going to let you take the first hit with the ax if you want. Aren't you excited?"

I look over at two big guys who shuffle into my room with axes, examining the wall like it is an obstacle they must tear down. Grandma would want revenge.

"We're going to need a one-on-one with Alyssa before we start the demolition," Frankie calls out. "We have a few more lines before she cruises out."

Vivian leans into me and hisses, "I would tighten that hideous bandana on your head first. You look terrible."

I see she is holding a plastic bag and motioning for me to take it. "I ordered it for you online," she says, softening. "Open it when the crew leaves."

I ignore her and turn back into my room, pushing past the two big guys to stand guard in front of the dresser, as if offering it protection.

"How am I supposed to get dressed with my room being taken over by these people? I'm a girl. I need some privacy."

"It's temporary," Vivian calls out. "We need you to cooperate right now."

"This *is* out of the ordinary," Mighty Mike adds, trying to help. "But it's all for the ratings. It will be a climactic episode and could earn a lot in revenue."

"If this is just for the ratings, I don't want to do it anymore. I thought we were doing it for *Grandma*."

Everyone is silent. And then Vivian pipes up, explaining that it is for Grandma, that she would love the makeover, and that this is how she would want it.

"Besides," she adds. "You can't quit."

"She's right," Frankie calls from behind the hole in the wall. "Not without parental consent."

I turn, peeking through the hole. "Did you just film that?" I reach my hand through, grabbing for the camera.

"Ahh!" the cameraman says, as my hand grips the lens.

Vivian yanks my arm away from the wall and bumps me into the dresser. Her grip is so tight that I let out a yelp, feeling her nails dig into my skin.

"We can renegotiate," Mighty Mike suggests, trying to relieve the tension.

I don't respond. I should have known to pack up earlier in case of an emergency like this. I start grabbing my things out of the dresser and piling them on the bed. I have no idea what I am doing, only that I want out of here.

"Alyssa can get notified when we're coming," Mighty Mike continues. "I think she deserves a break. The goal is to have a family-friendly television experience."

The skinny guy behind the camera nods, "This thing is your friend. You shouldn't want to attack it."

"No attacking the camera," Vivian repeats. "We're all on the same team here."

"I knooooow," I say, gritting my teeth and throwing my underwear on the bed, just to make the crew uncomfortable. I can't believe how much my arm hurts. I had no idea Vivian was that strong.

Frankie comes into the hallway and signals to the crew to give me space. As they shuffle out, I stuff the suitcase full.

"I'll trade rooms with you for a few days," Vivian suggests, sitting on the bed. "You can't abandon the show. You know how much this means to me."

"Your fans don't even know you have a daughter."

"They'll know now," she says, the hurt in her eyes. "You should open your present. The crew is gone." She gestures at the bag.

I reach out and open the bag. Stuffed inside I find a wig.

"What is this? Is it for me?"

"I know it's a bit long and dark, but we can cut it and get it styled to look just like your regular hair. I talked to Jodee and she agreed to it. I bet she can even put reddish colored highlights in it."

"I don't want to go back to that salon."

"Then we can go somewhere else. Alyssa, I think this would help."

Vivian is so excited, I imagine it's almost like she finally has an opportunity to make me over. I don't have a choice in the matter. Do I want to wear headbands for the rest of my life? Do I think I can stop pulling and grow my hair out really fast? It pains me to think about the months and years of my life I will spend growing it all back—that is if I can ever stop.

What I can't believe is how much this wig looks like Aurora's hair.

"Do you think it will really look natural?" I ask.

"It's the best thing I can do for you right now. We're going to keep getting you help. I know you can get better. It's a stressful time."

I nod in agreement, letting Vivian pull me into her arms. Even though I cannot stand her sometimes, she is still my mother. I put my head on her shoulder. I want to love and forgive her.

"You're my daughter. We're in this together." She glances around the room. "And this does means a lot to your grandma. This house is going to be gorgeous when it's over. We're all going to feel better."

I let out a sigh. "I'll stay, but no more surprises."

"Yes, yes," she says, but I don't believe her. "I'll make sure the crew knows your wishes." I nod, but I have a feeling she is being agreeable just to keep me quiet.

Vivian hands me the plastic bag. "This is all yours."

The wig is warm on my head a few days later in homeroom. I'm not sure if I'm just imagining it, but everyone is staring at me a second too long the way you do with Vivian. There is something different about me, whether you want to admit it or not.

The wig is way *better* than my normal hair. It is thicker and shinier, but the problem with the wig is that it's impossible to duplicate my real, natural curls. They are never the same day after day. The curls in the wig are more uniform.

I know people are noticing and I keep my eyes down more than usual. I'll probably be keeping my eyes down in the hallways from now on. It's too hard to have to face people and their questions.

When I pass Rachel, Toni, and Asher in the hallway, they are all smiles and I am relieved when no one asks me to explain.

Alex is at my locker before chemistry class, just like usual, and he also acts like nothing is out of the ordinary. "How do you think you did on the midterm?" he asks as we enter the classroom.

"I don't know," I say, glad to talk about something normal. "Probably bad."

"I don't believe it. You're one of those smart girls."

"What makes you say that?"

"Because you're amazing," he says. "Everything about you."

I try not to smile and find myself blushing and suddenly don't mind wearing the wig so much because I can hide behind it.

I don't want to admit my grade as I pick up my test and see the C-. It's the worst grade I've ever gotten. Lately, all my grades are C or below. I just can't study. Every time I sit with a book in my hand or the computer ajar, I turn to my hair.

After awhile, my brain shuts right off.

"I got a C+," Alex says. "Damn. This would not make my family proud."

"I didn't do so good either," I say. "By the way, how is your dad? Didn't you say he was sick?"

"He's still dying," Alex says. "Once you start, you usually don't stop."

"Alex, I'm sorry," I say, turning away from him as we talk. "I didn't mean to not be more supportive."

"It's all right. I've had plenty of time to accept it. It's just the idea of losing him and being the head of my family that scares me. You can't replace your own parents."

"You have your brother," I remind him.

"I have other siblings and relatives in Mexico, too, but it's just not the same. It makes me want to do the best I can with the opportunities here to help my family."

I wish more people were like Alex.

I think about the wig again and wonder if he has noticed. I look right at him, letting his dark eyes wash over me. He must see that something is different now.

"Can I tell you something?"

"I'm all ears."

I lower my voice, speaking so that no one else can hear. One of the forum users online has mentioned that telling our secrets can take the weight off of them, as long as you are careful about who you tell.

Since I cannot admit the whole truth, I tell Alex just a piece.

"I tried to dye my hair and these chemicals made it fall out."

Alex looks at me in surprise. "You dyed your hair? I can't tell."

I make a face that says *do not come any closer.*

"Well, it backfired."

"Oh no, that's not good," he says, like he understands, which is sweet. "One time I dyed this cat's fur with blue Kool-Aid and he looked like he was tie dyed."

"That's bad." I say. "But this is worse."

"Depends how you look at it. You are just the same to me."

I can't help but smile because I know he is sincere.

"Thank you."

"You're welcome," he says, like it's all very simple.

Halfway through class, Alex passes me a folded note with a drawing. It's a girl with one side of her head filled with curly hair flowing out of her scalp and the other half missing it.

Next to it he writes, *You're cute just the way you are.*

I hold the piece of paper and don't want to let it go. I imagine it with me for years to come, in all the places I will live and with all the people I will meet. It will keep me safe and comforted until the day I am old and pass away. I will keep the paper until it turns yellow and falls apart when you touch it.

chapter fourteen

The halls are swarming with students as we head to the gym. I follow Rachel, Toni, and Asher. We're having an afternoon assembly and pep rally about school safety, which Rachel explains is thanks to some guys trying to blow up the candy machines a few years ago.

"They do this assembly once a year now," she says nonchalantly as we make our way through the crowd. "Everyone knows it's kind of a joke."

"I see," I say, realizing my shoe is coming untied. As I lean down to tie it, a girl accidently trips over me.

"Oops," she says, trying to regain her balance and falling onto the floor, taking me with her. I feel my wig slide toward the right and grab it to pull it straight as quickly as possible.

"You can't just stop in the middle of the hall like that," she says, angrily.

I'm face to face with Jasmine in her cheerleader uniform with her skirt flipped up. She is with two other girls and they are carrying red and black pompoms. Both of the girls have their hair in matching high ponytails.

"I didn't see you," I say.

I realize this is the first time she has spoke to me since the day I tried to befriend her in the cafeteria.

"Watch it," she says, standing up and brushing her skirt down.

A few students around us have stopped to watch and we are at the center. I hear a few chords of "Fight! Fight!"

Jasmine leans toward me like she is about to help me up and picks up her pompoms instead. "You need to look where you're going and learn how to walk."

I hear the chords again. "Fight! Fight!"

But the last thing I want to do is fight.

"Hey, it's the girl in the wig," I hear someone in the crowd shout. Then he laughs and starts in on a new chant.

"Take it off! Take it off!"

Jasmine's face turns red and she draws away from the crowd.

I turn to find Rachel, relieved she hasn't been pulled away by the crowd. She grabs my trembling hand and we run down the hall, opposite the traffic of students.

Rachel stops at the nearest bathroom, guarding the door.

"You okay?" she asks as we step inside. "That was intense."

"Not really," I say, tears welling up as I stand in front of the mirror. I am trying to wipe away the tears, but they keep coming like a fountain.

Rachel meets my eyes in the mirror and we both look away. I don't want to state the obvious about the fact that I am wearing a wig and people were just chanting in the halls about it.

"This school is full of assholes," she adds, handing me a bunch of tissues. "I'm sorry."

"I'm ready to be home schooled," I say, carefully wiping my

131

eyes and making sure my fake lashes are okay. "Except I don't want to be home either."

"We can hang out here during the assembly if you want."

"I don't know what to do anymore," I say, feeling each quiet tear run down my face. I'm trying to control myself, letting in the pain, but I don't want to start sobbing in the bathroom.

Rachel puts her hand on my arm and nods. Then she grabs a tissue and hands it to me. "I know it's easy for me to say this, but if I were you, I would hold my head up high. People are always looking for someone to bully. It just shows how insecure people are. And stupid. But you've got me, and Toni and Asher. We all have your back. I know it's not much, but we would do *anything* for you."

"Thanks," I say with a sigh of relief. "That's like the nicest thing anyone has said to me in a long time."

"It's true. Come on."

I check myself in the mirror again, wiping away the tears. I'm surprised my eyelash glue has held on this long, but they look perfect, framing my red eyes. I know Rachel is right and I should go ahead and hold my head up high. I'm nervous to go back into the hallway, though, wondering what terrible thing will happen next. Rachel walks close to me, as if protecting me. I don't know how I'll ever thank her.

Just as we're about to reach the doorway to the gym, I see Alex with a backpack over his shoulder. Before he says anything, I know he has been waiting for me.

I glance at Rachel. "I'll see you inside."

"He has your back, too," she mouths to me with a smile.

"Hey," Alex says. "I was hoping I'd find you."

"I'm glad you did. I'm having a rough day. You don't even want to know."

"Well, do you want to skip the assembly and get out of here? Some friends and I are going to leave campus. We've got a car."

Technically only seniors are allowed to leave campus during the day, but Alex tells me we can hide in the backseat and get away with it. He says he wouldn't normally do this kind of thing, but he hates assemblies.

I hate them too. Especially now.

I bite my lower lip, unsure of how to decide.

Then Alex leans toward me and takes my hand, clasping his fingers around mine. His hand is warm and inviting and for the first time I am that girl holding hands with a guy at school. We are in front of the gymnasium door and I wish I could press the pause button because I feel so happy. It's like we're floating above everyone and I don't care where we end up.

"You're coming," he says, pulling me away from the gym and looking just as happy. "It's gonna be fun."

"Okay," I say, giving him a dazzling smile.

I can't believe a couple minutes ago I was on the verge of a meltdown and now I am in total bliss. Alex takes me to my locker to retrieve my bag and then whisks me down a hallway I've never been in before, with our fingers still entangled. We're running and laughing and suddenly I wish for the cameras from the show, witnessing this moment, capturing every angle.

We race down a staircase and at the bottom is a door that he props open. I breathe in the cool air outside. The sky is white and electricity is in the air.

What am I doing?

I send a quick text to Rachel as I catch my breath, wondering if she'll talk me out of leaving since it's against the rules. But her response is, *How exciting! Call me later.*

Then I think about texting Vivian, just to see if there is filming today that would give me an excuse to go home instead. I already know her answer is no.

We cross the parking lot to a tan, beat-up station wagon and Alex introduces me to a few of his friends. I know I shouldn't be here, but it's also exciting to have Alex bring me deeper into his world. His friends seem nice enough and pretty relaxed.

Actually, they are too relaxed.

When the car starts, all the windows in the car are down.

This immediately poses a problem for my hair. I am squeezed in tightly between Alex and another guy, my hand massaging the back of my neck, just in case I need to reach up. I don't think my wig can actually fly off, but I'm worried as the storm clouds get closer.

"Are you comfortable?" Alex asks, leaning toward me, and I realize his face is closer to mine than it has ever been before. I can actually feel his breath on my cheek. It smells like chocolate.

"I'm good," I lie, trying to play it casual, but my body is stiff.

The driver of the car lights up a cigarette and the girl next to him takes one too. They offer some to us in the back, but everyone says no, thank goodness. The smoke makes my eyes sting. At least when Vivian lights up a cigarette, she's careful to blow the smoke out the window. The driver and girl seem to be having a race to see how much smoke they can breathe on us.

Now my eyes are watering. I hope the extra glue I put on my false eyelashes holds up. I don't know how much more they can take today.

We make a sharp right turn onto the freeway ramp and I have a sudden desire to jump out of the car, as gusts of wind and smoke fill up inside. I feel trapped and start to breathe heavier, a strange sickening feeling coming over me. I hope a gust doesn't blow into my face, but I also don't want to draw attention to myself and insist we close the windows.

Be cool, Alyssa. Relax.

As if on cue, Alex reaches over and rolls up his window. We're driving right into storm clouds and the sky is now dark purple. I can't believe I didn't realize before what a bad idea it is to be outside right now. As his window rolls up, the car gets even smokier.

"How far away are the hot springs?" the girl in the front seat asks, blowing out a big puff. "I wonder if it's raining out there."

"Less than an hour," the driver answers.

"I can't wait," the guy next to me says. "I need some skinny dipping time!"

Did someone just say hot springs AND getting naked?

There is NO WAY I am getting near hot springs and melting my hair and makeup, let alone taking my clothes off. Suddenly, I am furious with Alex, and scoot away from him.

He glances my way carefully with those gorgeous brown eyes. I meet them and give him the dirtiest look I can muster. I'm sure he can see my anger. I have to get out of here NOW.

"You all right?" he asks.

I shake my head. "I'm getting car sick."

"Let me roll the window back down."

Before I can respond, large drops of rain are falling in between gusts of wind right on to my face and hair. My eyes start to water and I can feel the wig hair getting wet and tossed from every angle.

"Can we pull over at a gas station?" I plead.

"Sure," he says. "Of course. Hey guys, can we pull over at the next exit?"

I brace myself for each gust of wet wind and when all the windows are finally rolled up, we are at a gas station and I know I don't look right. As soon as we stop, I rush out of the car, feeling the wig mangled and smelling like smoke.

I hurry into the bathroom, composing a text to Vivian, asking her to pick me up because I'm sick and will explain the rest later. She'll be mad that I skipped school, but I don't care. Then I recall that she told me next time this happened she'd insist on more tests from the doctor. I think of Dr. Blah and delete the text. There is no way I'm stepping foot in a doctor's office right now.

I'm afraid they might lock me right up.

You're okay. Everything is okay, Aurora says. *I promise.*

Even if you get swept up in a wind storm.

Even if the rain pounds on your face and drowns you.

Even if you can't control what's going to happen next.

Suddenly, I remember I have the pills from the doctor in my bag. I reach inside and swallow one. I don't really know how fast they work, but taking one makes me realize how much I need help.

I wish it were possible to take a moment and undo it, like being an actor in a dress rehearsal and having another chance to get your scene right. If I had an undo button, I would push it right now and go back to school and be sitting next to Rachel on the bleachers, admiring my shoelaces and chewing a stick of gum. It would be nice to have a button like that, to avoid pain and tragedy. I guess it could also make you avoid good things, like love and euphoria and the bliss I felt holding Alex's hand.

You all right? he texts. *We're waiting for you. Rain has stopped.*

Doing okay. But thinking I'll get a cab and just go home.

Please stay. We're not going to the hot springs anymore. Just a drive. Okay?

He adds, *Sorry I didn't warn you. I realize you didn't pack your swimsuit. I didn't mean to make you uncomfortable.*

It's nice he thinks that this is my concern (or at least is playing along). Alex's worries are always so unlike my own. I forgive him immediately.

Then I see another text—this one from Kat.

Broke up with Josh. Call me ASAP.

You've got to be kidding me, I think, suddenly exhausted.

I dial her number, stepping out of the bathroom and wondering why I am hearing this news right now.

"Hey," she says, sounding surprisingly cheerful.

"Hey," I say, hesitant.

"Shannon and I went home early today to make sugar cookies for cheer practice. I'm trying to score points with the coach since I was late last week."

"Go Rancho!" Shannon shouts from the background.

I suddenly have nothing to say to her and want to hang up the phone.

"Everything else okay?" I ask, leaning against the wall.

"Oh… yeah… right. Josh was jealous of Steve, which is stupid because Steve was jealous of Matt. And Matt is not even cute. He looked like a comic book character and not in a good way. I don't know why I dated him."

"So you suddenly let Josh go?"

"I had to. I sent him a text. Do you want to see it?"

"You dumped him with a text?" I respond, amazed. Poor Josh.

"Oh, he'll get over it. They always do."

"Or he'll start worshiping you because he can't have you. I thought you guys were busy making babies and stuff."

"You know, I just don't want to get bogged down with one person right now."

"So he fell for you and now you don't want him?"

"I just want to keep my options open. No one can keep my interest for long. You know how I am."

Maybe that's because you are dating other people's crushes and destroying them one by one.

"Right," I say dryly. And then I lie and tell her I have another call and hang up.

Be right out, I text to Alex.

chapter fifteen

We drive until the city lights fade and darkness envelops the road. I have no idea where we are going, but I don't care. We stop and get pancakes for dinner at Denny's and since I don't have any money on me, Alex pays for both of us. Then we are travelling on a dusty, unmarked road where it is pitch black in the distance. I know that Vivian is busy with the last few weeks of the show and won't mind if I'm out for the evening. Plus, it's Friday and I'm tired of sitting home on nights like this one.

The windows in the car are down again, but we're driving slower and it's dark, so I don't mind as much. My wig is dirty and tousled from the wind and sand and cigarette smoke in the car and I'm sure it looks horrible. The car ride gets bumpier. I realize the sky has cleared and there are bright stars everywhere.

Somehow this makes everything better.

"There's a meteor shower tonight," Alex says, pointing up at the sky. "I think the storm made the air even clearer."

It's hard to tell from the moving car, but once we stop I see what he means.

Tiny white orbs fly across the sky. Some go from horizon to horizon, others you almost miss. Apparently this is what we've driven out here for, a fireworks show courtesy of the heavens.

Surprisingly, the rain didn't touch this place. It's dry and sandy. We've parked near a few boulders and when everyone gets out, Alex grabs a flashlight out of his backpack. It's a bit cold, so he hands me an oversized hoodie sweatshirt.

"Do you want to hike to the top?" he asks, motioning toward the rocks. "It'll be warmer up there and a better view."

"Sure," I say, joining him, as the rest of the crew stays near the car.

I move carefully, climbing up the rocks as Alex shines the flashlight below. Each step is like stairs, except totally uneven. My eyes adjust to the darkness and we reach the top, we are standing on a flat surface, wide enough to lie down. I peek over the edge and find the car below us with soft music coming out of the speakers.

"I've been wanting to show you this place," Alex says.

"Really?" I say, surprised. "You know about so many cool places."

"I like to explore. My brother and I hiked here when we first moved."

His flashlight turns off and a giant star skims across the sky, much bigger than the others.

"Wow," I say, feeling goosebumps.

"Here, lie down," Alex says. "It's the best way to watch."

I carefully tilt my head back, making sure the wig stays snug.

"There's Orion," he says, pointing to a constellation with three stars in the center. "And see that star?" he says, motioning toward another one. "It's not an actual star. That's Jupiter."

"Which one?"

Alex takes my hand, tracing it higher in the sky above Orion's belt.

"Then there's Sirius, near the horizon—the brightest star in the sky." He brings my hand toward the horizon, continuing to hold it. "It's called the dog star because it's part of Canis Major."

I smile. Alex is smart. I like being here with him in the darkness.

He points out other constellations and facts. I keep my head tilted away from him, just to be safe.

"It takes millions of years for the light from one star to reach us. It could even have exploded long ago and no longer exist."

"Like a ghost star," I whisper.

"Yeah," he says. "Many stars are dead and gone by now, but you can still see them for thousands of years. It's like their imprint remains forever."

"Do you ever think about how you'll die?" I ask.

"That's an odd question."

"I mean, if you could plan it ahead of time. Like if you were given a choice in your final moments or if you could see into a crystal ball."

"If I had a choice… I like good endings. Maybe mauled by a cougar or shot in the back by a terrorist. I want the whole package, the gut-ripping terror. I want to have never been more alive."

"Interesting," I say. "I've always thought dying in my sleep sounded nice."

"That's boring."

"It's pain-free."

"You've got all it wrong," he says. "You die without pain and you're dead already."

"How do you mean?"

"Well, if you don't go down with a fight you've already given up. Come on, think of something more exciting, Alyssa. Boring doesn't sound like you."

"Hmm. More exciting. Maybe an old-fashioned plane crash?"

"You can do better than that."

"A plane crash over a spurting volcano in Hawaii?"

Alex laughs. "Not bad."

"How about being in a sailboat, traveling the world. Maybe I would have the jewelry I make with me, selling it at different ports. The sky would look exactly like this, except there would be water everywhere below us." I hesitate, thinking how ridiculous this sounds.

"That sounds interesting. Go on."

"Well, it would be at night in the middle of the ocean. And this big storm is coming, like a monster in the dark clouds and the waves are getting higher and higher and splashing on to the boat. Instead of hunkering inside, I decide to stand out on deck and watch. Then I fight the storm and get tossed into the sea."

"Drowning," Alex says. "Now that's scary. You are brave."

"But there would also be sharks," I say, "waiting to eat me alive in the water."

Alex's expression changes and I suddenly remember the story about his mother and the shark tooth necklace.

I am such an IDIOT.

"I'm so sorry," I apologize. "I forgot about your mom. I can't believe I just made up something that horrible. I have a twisted imagination."

"It's okay," he says, his eyes shining in the darkness. "It

142

happened a long time ago. She's in a better place. She does have a good death story, though, doesn't she?"

I nod, feeling guilty for saying something so stupid.

"You know what I would do if I wasn't afraid?" he asks.

"What?"

"I would kiss you. Right now."

Then Alex leans toward me, closer than anyone has before. His hand wraps behind my neck and a warm breeze falls across us and I flutter my eyes closed. I know his lips are about to reach mine, but then I feel his hand again at the back of my neck. And then it touches the base of the wig, and I'm startled.

"Stop," I say, pushing him away.

I can't believe what has just happened. It's my second possible first kiss and here I am again, not ready and messing it all up. I want to cry and run and throw myself off the rock at the same time, but I'm in such shock that all I do is sit up, hugging my knees to my chest.

"What's wrong?" he asks.

I shake my head. There are no words. Both of our breaths are heavy and I'm suddenly aware of the heat rising up from the rocks.

"You can tell me," he says.

"No, I can't." I pull the hoodie sweatshirt over my head and tighten the hood so it covers my entire hair and face, with just a little area for my mouth and nose to breathe. "I just have this problem and I'm scared," I mumble.

"You don't have to be scared of anything with me. I've seen it all."

"Yes, I do," I insist, tightening the strings of the sweatshirt. "This is different. I'm not like everyone else."

"You're real," he says, trying to grab for the string on the sweatshirt to look into my eyes. "I'll be your friend no matter what. There has always been something different about you, but that's what intrigues me. You're just not like the other girls."

I realize he is sincere and ready to listen.

"I want to tell you," I say, uncovering my face. "But I can't."

"You can," Alex insists. "Or maybe you can text it?"

He pulls out his phone and writes something. My phone vibrates, indicating I have a text, and the screen lights up.

Why are you scared?

My hair, I type. *I don't want you to touch it.*

I won't. You told me about the wig already and I said I don't care.

It's embarrassing.

Don't worry. I don't care.

I need to tell you more about what happened. How I became this way.

Okay.

I pulled it out.

You pulled what out?

My hair. Hello!

Why?

I don't know.

That's not a big deal.

"Yes, it is," I say, putting the phone down.

"My friend's little sister does that. She doesn't have any eyelashes. I thought maybe you guys had the same thing, but like I said I don't care."

"I don't have any eyelashes either," I whisper. "I wear totally fake ones."

144

"They look good," he says, blinking at me. "You're not doing anything else bad to yourself, are you?"

"You mean like cutting?"

"Cutting, or anything."

"No, I've never done that. It seems like it would hurt."

"It does. I tried it once."

I let out a deep breath. I feel like I've jumped off a cliff into a giant abyss and even though nothing is catching me, the free fall isn't that bad.

"Why did you try it?"

"I like to try everything once, I guess."

"Well, I've definitely done the hair thing a lot."

"I won't tell anyone," Alex says. But can I just ask you one question?"

I nod and he asks, "Why?"

"Why?" I repeat, as if searching for the answer. "I don't know. I've just always been intrigued by my hair and I wanted to see it a little closer and I got carried away."

"Did something bad happen?"

"No, and that's two questions, Alex. Honestly, nothing bad has ever happened to me. I've been lucky, I guess. My parents are still together, sort of. I've never been raped or abused or anything. My life has been easy."

"That doesn't mean you don't have painful things."

I think of Josh and Kat in the tree house. And I think of Vivian and my father's girlfriend and how embarrassing it is to have a mother that resembles a Barbie doll and how she says mean things sometimes, yet I'm supposed to love her, and I do. I think of Jasmine and her friends in the cafeteria and how badly I wanted to

145

reach out and punch her pretty little face after she tripped over me.

"When bad stuff happens I pretend I don't care," I say.

"But you do care?"

"Maybe I do."

"You can't ignore the pain forever," he says. "You know, my brother and I have been shuffled around a lot and no one really cares what happens to us, except people who are far away. I'm not ashamed to cry a little. You know, no one has ever told me they love me?"

"No one? Not even your relatives or friends?"

"Nadie."

"That's sad."

Alex shrugs. "It is what it is. It's part of my life so I'm not going to deny it. I'm not going to ignore the pain because it's reality."

"I'd rather push it away."

"I think maybe you *like* it."

"I definitely don't like it, Alex. I'm not that kind of person."

I look carefully at him and then down at my hands, which have spent many hours inflicting a pinch of pain on my skin just for the reward of a single hair. I feel the rough skin on the end my middle finger, where I have sometimes pinched hairs to pull them out between that finger and my thumb. "Or maybe I do. I don't know anymore."

"You like it because it makes you feel alive."

Alex takes my hand, pulling it onto his chest. I can feel his heart beating and our breaths even together. I wonder if it is possible to do something that can make you feel both dead inside and alive at the same time. Because that, I think, is what happens to me.

chapter sixteen

I have it all planned out. Alex is going to be my boyfriend. He's going to take me to dances and we're going to sit on couches together and kiss while we pretend to watch movies. We're going to practice that thing called being normal and we're going to be experts at it.

It will make my crush on Josh look like child's play. I'm ready. I feel like I've waited a million years for someone to feel this way about me.

The morning after getting back from the desert, I still feel giddy. It feels like all these puzzle pieces coming together, including the idea of actually having pain and some problems in my life. I wouldn't say I want to cause any pain, but Alex is right. Painful things do happen, and they can shake you to the core. But they also can make you feel dead inside if they fester.

I think of all the time spent pulling and how my eyes are vacant and gray afterward. It's like I'm trying to kill something and rekindle it at the same time.

I've removed my wig, which is mangled and needs to be

washed, and I put on a knitted beanie that is navy blue with a button on the side.

"Hey, Alyssa," Frankie says, passing me on the stairs, his gray hairs sticking out from under his baseball cap. He is growing a beard, which I have learned is a tradition for the production crew. All the men grow facial hair each season and then shave it off when they're done filming.

"We're done early today," he adds.

"Good to know," I say, opening the door to my bedroom.

The bedroom makeover has just finished. It's about four times the size, thanks to knocking down the wall and combining it with the spare junk room. But now the walls are white, a white canopy hangs over a new full size bed with a white comforter and white pillowcases. There is a white dresser and white curtains and everything is so pristine I feel like I'm in a bubble.

"What do you think?" Vivian asks, admiring it from the doorway. "Do you love it?"

"It's very… white." I peek inside the closet where my clothes have been stashed and throw a few colored shirts on the bed. I wonder where that old dumpy quilt is, missing its personality.

"Those aren't dirty, are they?" Vivian snaps.

"They're clean," I reassure her. "I'm not going to throw dirty clothes on the new bedspread."

"Thank goodness," she says, letting out a sigh and brushing off some invisible dust from the dresser. "I think this room is divine and we need to keep it that way. You know, white is the trendy color right now. It goes with *everything*."

"It sure does," I say, noticing that it feels like all the personality has been squashed out of the place. "What color is your room going to be? Is the entire house going to be white?"

Vivian smiles mischievously, tapping her long fingernails on the dresser. "Well, Mighty Mike has this amazing idea. Since they're going to put the house on the market and offer the home buyers the furniture and whole nine yards from the TV show, we might play up on the Barbie angle."

"Meaning?"

"Pink. We're thinking a pink and white-striped bedroom with cool features and mood lighting. Something that would belong in a Barbie dream house, but it will be here in grandma's house." Her smile is so big I think she might be drooling.

"Which one is the kid's room? Shouldn't it be mine?"

"It's my show. Plus, you're hardly in any footage now, so no one will care whose room the pink one is. You know, your face gets washed out on camera so unless you want to start wearing lipstick, we won't include you. And with the situation with your hair, I figured you'd rather not have the attention."

"Okay," I pause. "Go back to your show then."

"Don't mock me. I think that even Mighty Mike is disappointed in your attitude."

Vivian keeps talking, and I try to tune her out. It's one thing to have a Barbie Lady mother, but giving her a Barbie bedroom in my grandmother's house? It's so weird I almost cannot believe it, and expect Mighty Mike to come running into the room saying it's a joke.

Suddenly she pauses. "Where is your wig? And why are you wearing that god-awful beanie?"

"It needs to be combed out," I say.

"Why? What did you do to it?"

"I didn't do anything." I take the wig out of my bag and show her, worried that I shouldn't let her take it.

"That thing looks and smells awful," she says, grabbing it from my hands. "It has lost all of its shine. We're going to have to get you another one. I can't believe you did this, Alyssa."

"Can't we just clean it? It got dusty in the desert."

"What were you doing in the desert? I thought you went to Denny's with your friends."

"I did both," I say quietly.

Vivian sighs. "I suppose we can clean it. But I want to be the one who does it because you might mess it up all over again. It might take me a day or two."

"What am I supposed to do in the meantime?"

"Wear a hat. Stop pulling. Help yourself a little."

"I can't wear a hat to school. Give me the wig back."

"No. I'm going to wash it for you properly. I think you take too many things for granted. I've spoiled you too much." Vivian clenches the wig in her hand and I know she won't let it go and my heart sinks because I don't have another option.

I think she wishes I would just disappear. Maybe she can throw the wig out and I'll disappear right along with it.

"I'm just a horrible person," I tell her, the anger bubbling up. "Maybe you should lock me up somewhere. Then you won't have to worry about me and my problems."

Vivian lays her icicle eyes on mine. "Would you really want that?"

"Sometimes," I say, half afraid that she could lock me up and that maybe it would be a relief.

"I could at least get a nicer wig," I suggest. "Or some hair implants or something. I'm sure they have stuff like that. Everyone at school can tell."

"The wig serves a purpose," Vivian says. "You've only just started wearing it and it will motivate you to grow your hair back. You can't change overnight."

"You change overnight all the time. You change in just a few hours in the hospital."

"That's none of your business to discuss."

"But it's true," I insist. "And *a lot* of people are discussing it."

"It's for the welfare of my career and company. Plus, it helped us get on this reality show, which is going to help pay for your college because I don't see you getting any scholarships in the state you're in."

"Fine. We don't need to talk about it anymore."

"Fine." Vivian folds her arms. "You're the one choosing to pull your own hair out. I didn't want to say this to you before, but it's disgusting. What do you think everyone back home is going to say when they see you? How can you do this to yourself? And to me?"

"You think it's a choice I'm making?"

"Of course it is."

"Sure," I say, just to agree with her. "One morning I woke up and thought, 'Gosh, I think I'll start ruining my life. What a great idea. Oh, and while I'm at it, I'll ruin yours too.'"

Vivian shakes her head. "I don't care if we have to handcuff your hands together, you have to STOP. How do you think it makes me look to my clients, and to the show, having a daughter who is doing stuff to herself?"

"They must think something awful of me and of *you*," I say, smacking my forehead.

"Don't talk to me like that," she warns, her blue eyes icy.

"How about if I stop pulling, you stop getting surgery. Deal?"

I put my hand out for her to shake it. Instead, Vivian's hand rushes straight up to my cheek, striking it.

My cheek burns like there is a lighted match against it. Suddenly, the only thing I can focus on is the spotless white carpet where we are standing.

"I'll see if I can special order you an eyebrow kit," Vivian says quietly, walking to the doorway. "They have three brushes and a couple different colors."

I wish I had never told her *anything*.

I decide to sleep on the couch that night. I find the old quilt in a bag in the basement and drape it over the cushions. I've kept out of Vivian's way for most the day and it's easy to ignore each other now, as she leaves the house with Mighty Mike for their stupid date. Here I am alone again, and now I have a case of insomnia.

I rummage through the fridge and take out a bottle of Vivian's wine, pouring myself a glass. I am desperate for sleep and hope it will relax me.

Then I down the glass and pour another one.

How fast does this stuff kick in?

I pick up my phone, reading over the texts.

I send one to Alex.

I tell him about Vivian and about what's going through my head. I text him more and more thoughts as I start on a third glass of wine, feeling dizzy. Even though he hasn't responded and must be sleeping, I keep typing, telling him things. I realize if I can admit my hair problem to him, I really can tell him anything.

And then I wake up on Sunday morning with a massive headache, vaguely recalling what I wrote to Alex.

What I have done?

My phone still has no new messages and I have a feeling I won't hear from him until Monday. Sometimes those things you think in the middle of the night are better off unsaid. Especially when you are all alone and getting drunk on wine.

When I get up for school the next morning, I am still in the same spot on the couch, which appears to be my new, permanent sleeping location. I wear the navy blue beanie to school with what is left of my hair in a ponytail. I realize this is a bit dangerous, but Vivian hasn't cleaned the wig yet, insisting it needs to be replaced after all the wind and rain and sand it was exposed to.

I hope the new one comes quickly.

Thankfully, most of the hair I've pulled is on the top, so I can still hide the damage pretty well as long as the top of my head is covered. I don't exactly have a choice. When I feel my real curls on my shoulders again, it's nice. I missed them.

I wait by my locker on Monday morning, pretending I am star of my own reality show, which includes no psycho Barbie Lady. Instead, it's just Alex and me and we are about to say our opening lines after the big scene on the rocks at night.

Yet for some reason I am nervous and playing with the ends of my hair.

He comes toward me is in the green button up shirt I remember from the day we first met. I give him a little wave.

Neither of us says a word as he walks with me to homeroom like usual. I half expect him to take my hand in the hallway, and my fingers brush past his, but he does nothing. For a second I wonder if he wants some space, or to walk ahead without me, but I push those thoughts far away.

I wonder if it was a mistake to send him all those texts in the middle of the night. I could just tell him it was an accident and a member of the film crew stole my phone. There must have been ten or so throughout the night.

Are you there?

I had fun with you in the desert.

We should go again.

 "So did you get in trouble for staying out late the other night?" I ask. "Or didn't Uncle Ringo know?"

"He trusts me. He knows about the spot."

I want to feel more alive, you know?

I'm getting drunk right now. By myself. I'm cool like that.

I wish you were here.

 "My mother didn't say anything either. She was probably glad to get rid of me. They're doing the final touches on the house. She is all wound up and bitchy right now."

Alex sticks his hands in his pockets. I try not to care that he is still not holding my hand.

"Is everything okay with your mom?" he asks.

"It's just the usual."

It sucks to have to hide myself. I'm tired of hiding all the time.

But I'm afraid I might have this problem for the rest of my life.

"You're going to get in trouble for that," he says, gesturing at the beanie and keeping his voice down. "Where is your wig?"

"It's getting washed," I say, which sounds totally ridiculous.

"That hat is against dress code."

"I know," I say, even though I completely forgot. "Do you think this really counts as a hat? I mean, it's more like a scarf or piece of yarn just thrown together into a round shape."

"I don't know," he says. "Just be careful who sees it."

"I'm not worried," I say, because I really don't feel worried at this moment. Whenever I'm with Alex, my worry dissolves. "You know, if I can sail around the world and live on a boat, and even die in a storm, I'm sure I can wear this thing on my head and get away with it."

There is something else you need to know.

I think that pain can make you feel alive, but so can pleasure.

"I'm sure you can," Alex says, and I can see that he has faith in me. As we're going toward my homeroom class where we'll part ways, he suddenly turns the other direction. "Hey, I need to grab something out of my locker. I'll catch up with you later."

"That's okay. I'll come with you. I don't mind."

I like you. You know that, right?

You might want to sit down because I am silly right now.

Are you sitting yet?

Alex is especially quiet and I wonder if he is tired today. When we reach his locker, I stand close to him, twirling one of the bracelets on my wrist. Alex pulls a long, green extension cord out of his locker and starts winding it around his arm to carry it. I am watching him, feeling at a loss for words.

Then some girl bumps my elbow with her backpack, startling me and I bump awkwardly into Alex. Sometimes I truly think I am invisible at this school.

I am suddenly aware that Alex is different today. Maybe I obsessed about our conversation in the desert more than he did.

155

I've never said it to anyone either, so here goes:
I more than just like you. I love you.
There, now someone has said it.
It makes me feel happy to be the first one to tell you.
I love you, I love you, I LOVE YOU!

I swallow and wonder if I said something terrible.

Alex shuts his locker door as the bell rings. "We have a quiz in chemistry today, remember? I have to get my grades up in that class. I want to go to college some day."

He starts walking, this time far ahead of me. As soon as he is out of reach I realize he hasn't even stopped to glance behind. I wonder if I wrote something entirely different in the text, or if I'd blacked out and typed a bizarre message, like *I love poo*.

My legs carry me toward him like I'm on a moving sidewalk and I surprise myself and grab the back of his shirt. "Wait," I say. "Where are you going? I thought you were walking me to class."

I am aware of students passing us and I definitely don't want to make a scene. I lower my voice, letting go of him and continue to walk, keeping my eyes down. "I thought the other night meant something. I thought you liked me. Didn't you read my texts?"

Alex shakes his head. "Yes, but I don't know how to respond."

"Well, I do. I know what I feel for once."

"Everything has changed," he says.

"Everything? Doesn't it matter what I said? Or do you think I'm a freak now?" I swallow a lump in my throat. "That's it, isn't it? You can't handle the truth."

"Alyssa," Alex says. "You know I care about you. You're my closest friend here. I'd ask you to be my girlfriend, but there's a problem."

"What is it?" I ask, my voice shaking. I think about the beanie and how ridiculous it must look and how Vivian took my wig away and I feel totally screwed without it.

"There is something you have to know," he says, putting his arm around my shoulder. It feels like a gesture from someone who sees me as just a friend.

"Oh god," I say, realizing he must like someone else.

"My dad died on Friday night."

My heart sinks. "I'm sorry," I mutter, feeling ashamed for thinking it was all about me. "I had no idea. You never talk about him, so I forgot how bad it was."

"It was bound to happen. But the thing is now I have to go to the funeral and then come finish tests and pack up. I'm moving to Mexico City. My family needs me there. I'm not sure for how long. It could be a couple months, or a couple years."

"Well, I'm leaving, too," I say.

"Fine. We're both leaving."

"I'm glad we cleared that up."

"I'm sorry, too," he says. "I shouldn't have spent so much time with you here. I didn't mean to turn this into something bigger than it is."

He says all this and then shakes his head and turns a corner.

I am crushed.

I don't even know if crushed is the right word. More like bulldozed, crushed, and meat-grinded. I have a sense that I have done all this before. My heart is a piece of rubber that has folded into itself and swallowed me into a black hole.

"Excuse me?" a girl says. I recognize her from homeroom. "Don't wear that hat to class. You'll get detention."

"This thing?" I touch my head, playing innocent again and

wondering why I've ceased to be invisible today. "Ah, no one will even notice." I push the beanie further down over my forehead, trying to convince myself.

I am so disoriented from Alex's news that I feel like a walking zombie. I step into class expecting to put my head down and daydream in the back row.

Big mistake.

Somehow the only empty desk is next Jasmine. Then I hear her voice. "You know, you can't wear that hat in here."

"I *know*," I say. "I have an exception."

"An exception?" she asks. "I'm sophomore class president and I don't have an exception. If I can't wear a hat in here, you can't either. Right?" She glances at her friends for reassurance. They nod in agreement.

"I'm wearing it today," I say, feeling the heat rising off my neck. I'm sure a giant rash is forming.

"That's not fair," she whines.

"A lot of things aren't fair," I mutter. "Who cares?"

"Why can't you take it off? What is your problem, anyway?"

"I don't have a problem."

Now my heart is pounding and I can feel it in my ears, the blood pumping into my head, through all my veins. I know I shouldn't do it, but I lift my middle finger up, pushing it against my cheekbone. I pretty much want to give this finger to everyone right now.

"Excuse me?" Jasmine says. "What is your name?"

I roll my eyes, not surprised that she has to ask. "My name is Alyssa," I mutter. "What's yours?"

"I know you," she spews. "And you don't know what you're

158

doing, Melissa. You don't want to mess with me. Not in the hallway or in this class. I can ruin you in a second."

The way she says this makes me angry in a way that is foreign and scary. "Go away, please." I drop my finger and face the front of the room, realizing we are about to cause a scene.

"Hats are not allowed and you need to follow the rules," she says even louder. Then she repeats herself, forming each word slowly so everyone stops what they're doing and listens.

"You… need…to…follow…the…rules."

Mrs. Boyer stops and notices us. Homeroom is pretty much a time to get caught up on homework and get the easiest A of your life. But now Jasmine and her friends have all the attention on me.

"Mrs. Boyer," she whines. "Melissa is wearing a hat in class today."

I am now in a nightmare and only have one option.

I bolt from my desk and into the empty hallway. I half expect someone to jump me, but it's peaceful and quiet, full of lockers and bits of paper on the floor.

In one breath it hits me just how bad things have become.

Soon, I am never going to see Alex again. I told him I *love* him and he couldn't even respond like a normal person. Maybe I made it all up in my head or the wine got to me. I've made enemies twice over with the queen of the school.

They all know I am the girl without the hair, if they didn't already.

Is this what Alex meant about pain making you feel alive? Because I don't want ANY of it.

Rewind. Rewind. Rewind.

chapter seventeen

"Live from the flickering lights of Sin City, this is Mighty Mike and the Barbie Lady with the final episode of Viva Las Vegas *Kicking it at Grandma's House*. We've seen a major home transformation this season, taking this place from barnyard bleak to modern and sheek."

"I couldn't have asked for more," Vivian gushes, in a plastic pink dress with knee high boots that make her resemble a 20-something. "This team did a fan-tabulous job."

"Fan-tabulous, it is," Mighty Mike adds.

I am holding up cue cards for Vivian and Mighty Mike. It's my new role for continuing to participate in the show, if you call it that.

"Grandma would love it," Mighty Mike chimes in. He introduces some of the behind-the-scenes team who collaborated to destroy Grandma's house. Everyone is high fiving and cheering on the white walls and modern impersonal furniture. There isn't an ounce of personality left in here.

Part of me is thankful for the distraction.

Every time I hold my phone I think about Alex and our text messages and conversations stored inside. He has left already, gone to the funeral and I haven't heard a word from him since our confrontation in the hallway.

I don't think I've ever had anyone disappear so completely.

It feels like I've had a breakup with my almost boyfriend, which may be worse than the real thing. At least with an actual boyfriend you get to have memories of making out and being together and maybe even having him love you back. This is more like a boyfriend from a TV show where I felt something and got to experience it, but never completely.

Sometimes I wonder if I am better off with a guy who lives behind a screen—movies, TV, online, in my imaginary world, whatever—because real love is too hard. It's much too unpredictable and scary. When big things happen from behind a screen, it's just an empty box with circuit boards firing and the intensity can fill me up and I can grip my chair and go for it.

Love. Grief. Despair. Passion. Pain.

I can let it flow into me like an IV and then switch it off.

"The best part of this house has yet to be revealed," Vivian says with her icicle eyes. "Let's find out what surprises await us upstairs."

"Yes, and we will do that right after this important message. Stick around." Mighty Mike points at the camera and gives me a thumbs-up. I drop the cue cards.

"Alyssa," Vivian orders. "We don't need your help anymore. You're excused for the night."

I wonder where she wants me to go since I *live* here.

"I'd like to see the upstairs room, too," I say, because I am curious. Plus, if Vivian wants to get rid of me I want to stay longer. I've never seen her happier. She is so happy that she even washes my wig and gives it back to me. I am wearing it again and suddenly wondering if I'll be wearing it for the rest of my life.

The thought makes me weak inside. I never thought much about my hair before, other than wanting to grow it long, and I took it for granted. But now that it's gone I feel like two different people. One of me is pretty on the outside, but the other, unspeakable.

Upstairs, the Barbie bedroom is just as gaudy and over the top as expected. They've decorated it with a pink chaise lounge chair next to a bearskin rug with a fake fireplace. The queen bed resembles a Barbie Corvette with a disco ball above and mood lighting that casts white orbs around the room. And of course, the pink and white striped walls.

Vivian expectedly screams and says she wants to live here forever, which of course we can't do since the house is going on the market.

That's when I look at her and wonder again what kind of psychological disorder *she* has.

"Congrats, my lady," Mighty Mike says embracing her off camera and spinning her in his arms. "I'm so glad you love it. It's going to be a bummer to leave this place."

"I know," she whines, playing with the suspenders on his blue jeans. "I don't want to think about it."

"It's a good thing we have more partying to do!"

"Yes!" she says.

"By the way," Mighty Mike says, facing the crew and me. "Mark your calendars for two weeks from today. We're having the wrap-up party at my makeover mansion headquarters."

A few crew members whistle and Mighty Mike points at me. "You'll be there too, Alyssa. Right?"

"Uh, yeah," I say, wondering if there is an alternative.

"Sweet." Mighty Mike swoops Vivian up in his arms.

"Alyssa," Frankie says, taking me to the side. "You know this is all just part of the show, right?"

"What do you mean?"

"Your mother and Mighty Mike acting like hornballs together."

I cannot believe Frankie has just said hornball in a sentence. "They're not even on camera. So it seems pretty real if you ask me."

"No," Frankie says shaking his head. "Just between you and me, Mighty Mike does this with the ladies from every season. He would have hit on you too if you were over eighteen. I think they're practically going to have to hire a marriage counselor if the show continues."

I glance at Vivian again and then back at Frankie, needing a break from it all. "I need a favor. Can you give me a ride somewhere?"

"Sure, the filming is about over. Where are we going, Miss Alyssa?"

"Can you just be my taxi for a little while? I'm not sure yet."

I quickly pack my suitcase with clothes and my overnight stuff and slip out the door with Frankie. This all feels strangely familiar and yet I remember I've been doing it for years when I'd to escape to Kat's house.

This time I give him directions to where Alex lives.

When we pull up to the curb the upstairs windows are dark and I imagine Alex sleeping and me crawling into his arms just like Aurora and Hoffman do. He wraps his arms around me and realizes that he does love me after all.

163

"You can stop here," I say to Frankie, opening up the car door. "Wait for me, okay?"

I'm not sure why I'm here, only that part of me doesn't believe Alex is gone. I approach the house, walking on the dying grass, and peek into the front window.

There is one lone lamp in the center of the living room and an older man in a chair watching TV. Uncle Ringo. His back is to me and I wonder why he isn't at the funeral too. I hesitate and ring the doorbell, but he doesn't come to answer and then I remember how Alex said that nothing can come in through the front door and that you're supposed to take a shower first before going inside.

I push the doorbell again and again, but Uncle Ringo doesn't move from his chair. I look up at the stars, so far away above the city lights, and realize, suddenly, that I shouldn't be here.

Alex is gone. There is no button for yesterday.

"Anybody home?" Frankie yells from the truck.

"No," I say, realizing I don't know when I'll hear back from Alex. I can't control any of this, including his feelings or mine or where he is right now or what all of this will become. All I have is the uncertainty. It's all I've ever had, I guess.

"Let's go," I say. "This place gives me the creeps."

I tell Frankie how to get to Rachel's house and when we arrive I carry my suitcase to the front door just the way I used to do when Kat's family would take me in.

"It's going to be okay," she says, answering it and giving me a hug. "You can stay here tonight."

"That sounds good," I say, letting her comfort me.

I spend the night at Rachel's and everyone is nice and normal, just the way a family should be. Her mom makes us wheat-free pancakes in the morning and her little sister is doing watercolors and the dog does its usual loops around the living room furniture.

In the morning, Vivian texts me that she has booked a hotel suite downtown, with the house on the market soon, and asks if Rachel's family will take me in for the next few weeks.

I'm taken aback and text her, *I can't ask to stay here a few weeks. I've never even done that with Kat.*

Well, I just thought it might be more fun for you, she writes back. *I'm working a lot right now and I would hate to leave you here night after night.*

Sometimes I don't know why Vivian bothered bringing me.

What am I supposed to tell Rachel? I've only been over here a few times.

Just ask Rachel to talk to her parents. Tell them you need a place to stay. Don't ask—tell.

Okay, I'll do it, I write.

Great. Let me know what they say.

I put my phone down. It's confusing to hate someone you're supposed to love so much. I do love Vivian, but right now I think she is going mad and taking me with her.

I'm not sure how, but I convince Rachel to ask her parents and they say yes and I'm not homeless after all. Rachel's family is friendly and welcoming, giving me my very own chair at their dinner table, and I never want to leave.

I stop pulling for the first few days at Rachel's and then when I finally do break my stopping record, I make up for it with a vengeance.

I wear my wig until I fall asleep and pull it right back on in the morning. The wig has also made it easier, in an odd way, to let myself pull even harder with the hair that I do have left. This time

165

every hair gets flushed into the toilet, gone forever.

Part of me hopes I might actually get caught at Rachel's house or that someone finds the hair and asks what happened, but most people wouldn't dare ask that kind of question.

The crown of my head has bald patches *everywhere*. I resemble a man who is losing his hair and I cannot believe I did this to myself and want to do more.

The problem is, if I don't pull I feel like I'm going to explode.

I skip homeroom for the week, taking the usual bathroom stall by the window and imagining what it would be like to escape from everything. Other girls come in to smoke next to the window and I think about asking if I can have a cigarette too, but it reminds me of Vivian.

After a while it gets to be too much and I have to leave the bathroom, not wanting to smell the smoke.

That's when I run into Mrs. Boyer in the hallway.

"Alyssa," she says, surprised. "Are you skipping homeroom again? Let's get you back to class. I was just working on grades and your attendance rate is low. You're already at an A- and I'm about to drop it to a B if you don't come to class again."

I wrack my brain for an excuse, but the smoky smell from the bathroom has gone to my head and I can't think of anything. I haven't seen Jasmine since the day I ran out and hopefully she will leave me alone this time. I'm sure she has plenty of other girls to pick stupid fights with.

Yet as Mrs. Boyer holds open the door for me to come into homeroom, I am suddenly extremely nervous. My head feels hot with the wig, and I push the artificial hair over my shoulders, trying to be brave and hold my head high.

I sit a few desks from Jasmine, behind a couple nerdy guys, who thankfully don't take much notice of me.

I open up my chemistry book, trying to read it, but the words run together. It reminds me of Alex. I see one of the doodles he drew for me in the margin, with a dolphin jumping out of the sea wearing a cape. I still haven't heard a word from him and I wonder if he is still alive and thinks of me.

I am thinking about him and the funeral and what it must be like in Mexico burying a dad you barely knew when a note lands on my desk. Someone has folded it into an airplane.

I see my name on it and I raise my head.

Are you wearing a wig?

I sigh. Haven't we covered this already?

I glance at Jasmine, unable to help myself, but I must be old news to her. She doesn't even turn her head. Then I realize there is a hand at the back of my neck, grasping the wig hair. I jerk forward, realizing it's the guy behind me.

"Feels real," he says.

"Let go," I say firmly.

"But it's not your hair," he says. "It's a wig, right?"

"Who cares? Let go."

"Everyone is talking about it online. Someone started this rumor. You mean you haven't heard?"

He shows me his phone with a website open, making sure Mrs. Boyer doesn't catch him, and I see the following statement and comment:

I think this girl in my homeroom is wearing a wig. Her name is either Melissa or Alyssa. Has anyone else noticed?

Yes. Totally weird.

She could have a disease.

Fake hair? Eww gross.

I swallow hard.

I know I can't run out of class now, and yet I feel sick like I might throw up. I'm better off not hearing the things people are saying behind my back. It is sometimes better just to be naïve.

I scoot far down in my chair and pull out my phone to text Rachel. She immediately writes back, *Who cares what they think? You are brave and strong and beautiful.*

Then I text Kat, *I'm having a bad day and could use some help. You there?*

She writes back, *#17 Sexy Ben turned out to be gay. Feel any better?*

I smile in spite of myself.

Then Rachel sends me a link to a local support group for people like me. *I just found this. I think you should go. I can come with you if you want. Maybe your mom would come too.*

I'm sure my mom would love meeting more ugly weird people.

Come on! Stop putting yourself down.

You're right. I think it's a good idea. Thank you.

I put my phone away. There is nowhere to hide in this school, or anywhere really, but I realize that some of the strange looks from my classmates are actually sympathetic.

No one wants to be the girl who is different, yet as each person acknowledges me, glad they aren't being singled out, I feel this strength burning inside. It's unlike anything I've felt before.

It's like a fire has been lit in the center of me.

I lift my head up high and let them stare.

chapter eighteen

I am the youngest person in the group.

Everyone has brilliant ways to cover up the damage, from eyebrow tattoos to lash extensions to gobs of makeup. Amazingly, it's almost impossible to tell what anyone in here is hiding.

There are twelve women in the room, including hair pullers and one lady who picks the skin on her arms so hard that she has to wear long sleeves all year long. The meeting is held in the basement of a hospital, down four flights of stairs, past a maze of blue doors into a room with no windows. We can't talk about our last names or where we live. I just signed a confidentiality form and Rachel has to wait outside.

"We have a new member tonight," Susan, the group leader says. She is a psychologist who leads the meetings. "Let's do introductions."

Everyone turns their heads where I sit with Vivian at my side. As a family member, she is allowed at the meeting.

I am surprised Vivian wanted to be here, but then Rachel's mom found out about the wig and personally called Vivian. Now I am like the bad kid who is staying at Rachel's house and everyone is concerned about what I could do to myself next. And with Vivian's concern about her reputation, I'm sure this has made her even more delighted with me.

Insert extreme sarcasm.

I tried to explain to Rachel's mom that I'm not doing any serious harm, that I doubt I would ever cut myself, or anything dangerous. Yet she was so worried, it made me more worried.

"Hi, I'm Alyssa," I say, and I take a breath. "I'm fifteen and a sophomore in high school. My pulling has been really bad this year. And this concoction on top of my head is obviously not my real hair. People at school are noticing and I don't really know what to do."

A few of the members give me sympathetic nods, welcoming me.

Next to me Vivian is being extra quiet and her leg is twitching. She introduces herself, explaining that she is concerned about what this disorder is doing to me. I grab her leg to make it stop.

"As a mother, this is really hard to watch," she says in this strange voice, which I suppose sounds compassionate to other people. It doesn't really *seem* like my problem is hard on her. She still gets up every day looking perfect, goes to parties, stars on a TV show, and doesn't care if I live with her. I wouldn't dare say it, but part of me thinks she enjoys watching me suffer.

A few of the other women share their stories and listen. "I used to have the most beautiful hair," one says, her hair pulled back into a thin ponytail.

"You're still beautiful," another woman says, wearing a chin-length platinum blonde wig.

"Hair is everything," another woman says. "I have to keep this problem private at work and even with my family. It's not easy."

Another lady pipes up. "I'm getting married in a month. My goal is to have enough lashes so that I can wear mascara for the first time. My fiancé doesn't know what I do. I've been pulling since I was twelve, but I'll never tell him."

She pauses, turning to me. "I hope we're not scaring you."

I shrug. "It's not scary. It's nice to know I'm not alone."

A few of the women take off their wigs, which seems kind of liberating, but I choose to keep my head covered.

Susan, the leader, gives everyone a worksheet and we talk for a few minutes about things we all have in common, like a sensitivity to touch. Susan explains that pullers are often "tactile," which means when we touch things like soft fabric, the textures feel more rich to us than most people.

"It can be a wonderful thing," she says, "to be so sensitive to the world around you. For some of you, it might even be your gift."

I never thought of being sensitive as a good thing, let alone a gift.

"It can give you great intuition," Susan adds. "And because many of you feel and think things more deeply, you have the potential to feel more love and joy in your life and share these things with others. Speaking of sharing, we have a special guest here that some of you might recognize."

"I'm Jamie," one final woman says, sitting across from me. "I'm just visiting."

Jamie is a few years younger than the others with strawberry blonde hair that curls and falls across her shoulders. "I used to come to these meetings a few years ago when I was in high school.

171

Now I'm finishing up college and my hair has grown back, almost completely."

"Congratulations," Susan says at the head of the table.

I can't take my eyes of Jamie. She reminds me of me.

"I know these meetings are discouraging at times, so I like to stop by for moral support," she says. "I still consider myself a puller, except I no longer pull. I see the problem as a part of me, but now it's asleep. After a while you forget you ever had it."

"What else is different about your life now?" Susan asks.

"Well, I'm getting married," Jamie says with a smile. "But other than that, my life is not that different. I thought getting better would change everything, but it was just a tiny piece. I still have plenty of other problems." She laughs a little.

"But isn't there something special you've been doing in your spare time?"

"Yes," Jamie answers. "I've been invited to a special training camp for the Olympics. I'm a competitive swimmer. I missed out on my chance when I was in high school because I wasn't swimming, but now I'm back in the water and these possibilities are opening up. It feels like I'm playing a lot of catch-up right now in my life."

Everyone around the room nods and my mouth drops open.

"The best part was being able to swim again without feeling self-conscious. I missed it so much. I love the water."

Now my eyes are filling with tears.

"How did you stop?" asks Brandy, the girl with the thin ponytail.

"I had to dedicate myself completely just like I do when I compete. And I had to fail sometimes and start over again. The idea of 'stopping forever' is pretty hard. I think it's the word 'forever.'

You stop and think you're cured and then screw up again. It's kind of like an analogy for life."

Jamie continues. "So I started giving myself forgiveness hairs. Like, if I accidentally pulled one out after a few days or weeks, I wouldn't punish myself or pull more. I became aware of all the sensations and anxiety in my body and I started with the challenge of a month of stopping, which turned into a few months and a few years, and a few setbacks. And here I am today."

The group members ask Jamie a few more questions, but you can hear the doubt in their voices. Most of the women are older and you can see the years of giving up on their faces. Yet we are all here at this meeting and have a chance.

I'm afraid I might have this problem for the rest of my life.

Jamie's words go right to my heart, as if they are intended just for me. I am the youngest person in the room. I have my whole life ahead. I don't have to take this to the grave. Nothing is permanent—not a behavior, not a thought, not a feeling. Not even life. And it is a good thing.

Funny, that sounds like something Alex would say.

At the end of the meeting I exchange email addresses with Jamie. "Stay in touch, Alyssa," she says. "Be sure to keep coming to these meetings either here or in San Diego. It will help you. I know you're going to swim again and feel totally comfortable."

I hug her, wishing Vivian hadn't come with me. Having my mother here, for some reason, cheapens the experience.

"What did you think?" Rachel says as we meet her back at the car.

"It was good," Vivian says. "I think it's just what Alyssa needs."

"Yeah," I say, agreeing with her. "It was eye-opening."

"You're coming back to my house, right?" Rachel asks.

I look at Vivian, assuming that this is the plan. We are leaving Vegas in a couple weeks, with only a final wrap-up party for the show planned.

"Yes," Vivian says. "The hotel suite is actually quite small. I assume it's all right with your parents to keep Alyssa for now?"

"They're fine with it, I think," Rachel says.

I am disappointed that Vivian can let me go to Rachel's so easily, especially after a meeting like this one. Vivian may not be my favorite person in the world, but she is still my mother. I am suddenly homesick, but I'm not sure for where.

Instead of going back to Rachel's and dumping my tweezers, I stand in front of the bathroom mirror, just noticing how they feel in my hand. I really do have a sensitivity to touch, especially at the ends of my fingertips. I put the tweezers down, removing my wig.

I really hate looking at myself this way. What is left of my hair reminds me of a doll's head with hair that has been worn away. It's like something you'd find chewed up in the back yard by the neighbor's dog.

Even after hearing Jamie's speech, the urge is knocking, as strong as ever. I can't think it away. I can't tell myself not to feel it. It is as strong as a gunshot. So at this moment I pick up the tweezers, about to do an experiment. I watch myself methodically go after each hair. I have this sense that I need to pull—to get it out of my system—because I am about to do something truly crazy.

I open the bathroom cabinet and pull out an electric razor.

I plug it in and turn it on, buzzing the side of my head. What is left of my lovely curls falls to the floor.

Goodbye Alyssa.

I shave *all* of it, even the patches of hair I've never touched. It is gone in an instant. Once I finish, I wait for the panic, for my hands to turn into fists and break the glass because of everything I have done to myself in only a few months. Except I feel strangely peaceful, like I'm underwater and coming up to the surface.

I am no longer me, except I am still there.

I expect to see my dead gray eyes in the mirror, but instead it is like waking up from a coma. My cheeks are pink and glowing. My face is oval and more heart-shaped than I realize. My eyes, which I've been convinced are a blue-gray mutation, are a dazzling midnight blue.

They belong on a fairy.

I look powerful, feminine almost. I look like I could kick anyone's butt.

Bring it, Jasmine Petrovich.

I slip the beanie back on head, amazed at the sense of calm I feel. If I'm going to look into the mirror, I don't want to just see the wig that Vivian has chosen and the damage I've done. I want to see the girl behind the wig because she is who matters.

chapter nineteen

The night arrives for Mighty Mike's wrap-up party. It's the first time I have seen Vivian since the support group and she greets me with a kiss on the cheek from her newly enhanced lips. My wig is firmly on my head and I can feel her eyes taking in every strand, making sure not a hair is out of place.

We've parked the car at the curb and are being driven in a golf cart to the front door of a huge mansion.

"Could you please slow down?" Vivian asks the driver as he takes us along a winding path. We pass a flat wall that has a waterfall built into it. She turns to me. "Your hair isn't getting loose, is it?"

I run my fingers through the wig, feeling the water droplets pass through in air. "No, I think it's secure."

"Phew," she says.

Vivian doesn't know I shaved my head. It's my little secret. For some reason knowing I could whip the wig off at any second and scare the daylights out of her is amusing. With my long curly hair a memory I don't mind the wig as much. It is starting to feel like a natural extension of me.

Unfortunately, Vivian picked out my dress for the event and I didn't try it on until an hour ago. It's a leafy green color with ruffles on the chest and it poofs up in the back. I think it's a size too small and I feel like I'm dressed up as a Romaine salad. Even with my sexy black high heels I feel out of sorts already.

"You could have at least gotten your makeup done with me," Vivian says, as if sensing my discomfort. "This party is kind of a big deal." Naturally, she is wearing a fancy red dress with sequins, red high heels, and a glamour Barbie hairstyle with her hair piled on top of her head by professionals at the hotel salon.

"I was watching a movie with Rachel. And then I didn't want to miss dinner. Her mom made us homemade macaroni and cheese."

"That sounds like a thousand million calories."

"It was good."

"Suit yourself," she says. "There are going to be photographers and news people and important guests at this party. I suppose they can always Photoshop you if there's a problem."

"Whatever works," I say, shrugging off the insult.

"Believe me, you want to look good."

I want her to shut up.

"Helllooooo ladies," Mighty Mike booms from the front door as we pull up. He is in a full-on penguin tuxedo, with cameras set up behind him and half of Las Vegas in the foyer. "Welcome to the after-party!"

Vivian kisses him lightly and he explains that the footage for the party might be used for a bonus episode, depending on the show's ratings.

Photos snap as we walk into the foyer with high ceilings, a marble floor, chandeliers, and a grand staircase. It almost reminds me of what the White House might look like inside. Vivian poses next to a statue wearing chainmail and her dazzling smile lights up the room. People are swarming the entrance for a chance to get a photo of her.

"Your mother is spectacular," one of the partygoers tells me. "Did she really just have surgery a month ago?"

"What's it like being the daughter of the Barbie Lady?" another asks. "Do you think you'll follow in your mother's footsteps?"

Oh my god. I have to get out of here.

I do a quick assessment of the room and spot a doorway. I walk toward it purposefully, hoping no one will notice. Beyond it is a long hallway with dark wood panels and flickering lights that resemble candles. It reminds me of something you'd see in a castle. Framed photographs line the hallway.

"I see you've found the memorial wall," Frankie calls out behind me.

"Is that what this is?" I ask, turning toward him. "I needed a break from the insanity."

"Already? It just started."

"Speak for yourself."

Frankie goes on to explain, "These are the photos of all the grandparents whose houses we've renovated. Your grandmother is up here somewhere."

"Dead people. Interesting."

"Here she is," he says, gesturing. He points out a montage of black and white photos of my grandma when she was a teenager. One is of her winning the Miss Dairy Queen pageant with a sash around her neck and a cow at her side that appears to be constipated. I bet Vivian didn't pick that photo out.

The next one has her in cowgirl clothes, waving a hat in the air. I think she is riding a mechanical bull, although I'm not sure if they had those back then.

"She looks like a lot of fun," Frankie says.

"Like a free spirit," I say. "Just the kind of girl that would want her house turned into a giant marshmallow."

"More color may have been appropriate, but I didn't make the plan." He holds up his hands. "I just follow orders."

"Well, maybe I can order you to get me a drink."

"Of course, madam. What would you like?"

I smile and ask Frankie for some punch and survey the partygoers from the safe space in the hallway. Vivian is nursing a cocktail and soaking up the attention with every fiber of her being. She is leading a parade of people and photographers into another room.

"At least it's officially the last night," Frankie says, bringing back a drink for me. "You know, no one is going to care what your mother does to herself when this thing is over. Maybe you should come and enjoy the attention too."

"I'd rather not."

"Suit yourself, kiddo. I'm sure we'll see you soon."

Frankie turns around, heading back into the crowd. I'm left in the hallway, wondering where I could camp out for the next few hours. Since the foyer has cleared out, I decide it's safe to explore. The grand staircase is beckoning me and I climb it, listening to the tapping of my high heels against marble floor. When I reach the top, there is a giant mirror.

I turn away.

Sometimes it's better not to face the mirror. Instead I follow another dimly lit hallway with large intricate wooden doors.

179

I open one of the doors, curious. The room is decorated from floor to ceiling with gold and yellow wallpaper and a bed with a canopy. "Wow," I say to myself, walking toward the bed. "Now this is what I call a bedroom."

I flop back on the bed, pushing the wig aside to scratch the top of my head. The hair on my head is very short and fuzzy now. I've been tempted to pull it, but have managed to go the week without a single hair. I'm proud of myself. Ever since the support group, I've had this seed of hope inside. I have to hold on to it.

Having my head shaved is a relief, but it also leaves me with a few questions: *Am I going to be hiding like this forever? Is this just the beginning of telling lies to people?*

I shift my focus to a window in the corner of the room. Just when I am getting used to the wig, there are other parts of me I know I keep covered.

Vivian is right about one thing. It's going to be impossible to keep this from my friends back home. They are definitely going to notice the difference and I don't think it'll be good. I may be making an entirely new group of friends.

And that's okay too. Sometimes you outgrow your friends.

My phone buzzes with a text, no doubt, from Vivian. I roll over on my stomach pulling the phone out of my purse to respond. She probably needs me for a photo shoot. They should have made a paper doll cutout instead.

Are you there? Alex asks.

I stare at the screen, surprised, and can't help but smile.

Yes, I'm here. Where are you?

In the neighborhood wondering where you are.

It's good to hear from you.

180

Do you want to hang out?

I let out a laugh, shocked by what I'm reading. Then I stand up and pace around the room, unsure of how to respond and I find myself facing the window. That's when I realize the yard is huge. About half a football field away is a lit up oval-shaped swimming pool. It is deserted. And familiar.

Oh my god. I've been here before.

I start texting furiously.

I'd love to hang out. How about a swimming lesson?

Where are you?

I giggle. *Your favorite pool. I'm looking at it right now.*

What pool?

You know the one.

What are you doing there?!?

I know people who know people. I'm a guest here tonight.

You're just like that. Always amazing me.

So, are you coming over or what?

A rush of adrenaline shoots through me and I leap off the window seat. I don't even have a swimming suit, but it's dark outside and I want to keep my promise. I grab my purse off the bed, wondering how I'm going to swing this idea with the mansion full of people. But if Alex wants to do this, I'm in.

As I slip back out of the room, I make up a story to keep my nerves down.

Closing the bedroom door. *Once upon a time there was a girl in a castle.*

Down the hallway. *Who needed to escape before she became the prisoner.*

At the grand staircase. *So she fled to the forest to slay the unknown.*

I remove my high heels at the back door and walk through the damp, cool grass, passing spotlights and rock waterfalls and stone-carved gargoyles. I pass rows of palm trees with leaves that cast eerie shades on the ground before me. I try to ignore the feeling that I am being watched.

"Hi there," Alex says, coming out of the trees and meeting me at the pool gate. He is wearing long shorts and a white t-shirt and carrying a flashlight. He shines his gorgeous dark eyes at me, making my heart swell.

"You got here fast," I say, realizing the last time we faced each other was at school.

"You too."

I wonder if I should say something about how awkward it was and that I was probably drunk when I texted him those words. But somehow having him close to me again, I feel a rush of emotion and wonder if maybe I do love him after all. Maybe it's even okay if he isn't able to love me back. There is something so sweet and vulnerable about Alex that makes him easy to love.

"Are you still moving?" I ask.

"Yes," he says, taking a deep breath. "Sorry. I just had to see you again. I never got to say a proper goodbye."

"When you leaving?"

"My flight is tomorrow and I don't have a return ticket this time. I'm not sure how long I'm going to live there."

I swallow hard, the reality of what he is saying hitting me. He is literally here for a couple hours just to turn right around and walk away. Part of me wants to tell him to leave now. Why bother creating a memory when it is the last one?

"I'm glad we're doing this right now," he says, taking my hand, as if sensing my discomfort. "I won't be gone forever, you know."

"Let's just do this, okay?" I say, leading him toward the pool, which is lit up with green and blue lights.

"Are you going to give me a lesson or some tips?" he asks.

"Oh yeah, but first I want to get in and swim a little. It has been ages."

"You wearing that?" he asks, gesturing at the lettuce dress.

"Yes, I am. I knew there was a reason I hated this dress so much."

"I'll wear my clothes too," he says. "I don't own swim trunks, so it's perfect."

Even with the pool lights, it is dark out here. It will be hard for anyone to see us unless they come all the way back, which is unlikely. The only sound is the trickling waterfall, next to the mermaid statue. She appears to be watching our every move with her frozen stone eyes.

The next question is what to do with the wig. I twist it into a bun and wrap a rubber band around it, hoping it will stay. When I finish, Alex is already in the water making bubbles with his t-shirt.

"Here goes nothing," I say, stepping down the stairs in my dress. I slide my hand down the metal handrail, feeling the water hit my ankles, then my knees and my thighs and the edge of my dress and all the way up to my hips and stomach. I laugh, hardly able to believe what I'm doing.

I make it up to my chest, where Alex is standing.

He tries a weak doggie paddle toward me, but struggles to keep his body afloat, kicking so hard that water splashes up on the concrete.

I spread my arms out and glide to the deep end, feeling the water envelop my body. I want to go under, but I don't dare with the wig. I turn away for a moment, pulling it closer to my head.

"You okay?" Alex asks.

"Fine," I mumble. "Just thinking about stuff."

"I thought you were ditching me because my swimming sucks."

"Come on. I would never do that to you."

At the deep end, I remind myself of the day I shaved my head and how I resembled a fairy and how blue my eyes were. Then I take the wig off, feeling the cool air on my skin.

I swim back toward the shallow end, this time ducking under and swimming below the surface with my eyes open. When I reach Alex, I raise my head, feeling the water dripping down my neck.

This is the first time I have let anyone see me without my wig.

"Look at you," he says, stepping closer to me. "It's cute."

"You don't have to lie."

"I never lie," he says. "Ever."

I turn to float on my back with my toes in the air, feeling the material from the dress under me. I notice the stars. They are smaller tonight.

"Do you know how to float on your back?" I ask, flipping over and standing in front of Alex.

"I don't know. I've never tried it." Alex turns on his back and immediately sinks. "I can't do it."

I place my hand on his lower back. "Yes, you can. Just relax."

He tilts his head back and spreads his arms wide, as if making a snow angel. I hold him up with both hands. Then I slowly move my fingers away, until only my pinky fingers are holding him. "You've almost got it," I whisper, watching him grow completely still. He floats for a couple seconds on his own.

"Wow," he says, letting his feet touch the bottom again. "I

think that was the most relaxed I've been in my entire life."

"Let's go below together," I suggest. "Want to?"

I show Alex how to blow bubbles and then we hold our breath at the same time and dip under, keeping our eyes open below the surface. He makes a funny face. I blow him a kiss. I motion for him to try and sit at the bottom with me. It's only four feet deep, but he keeps floating up. I stay three times as long, as he goes up and down.

"Have you ever been kissed?" he asks, as we come up to the surface.

I cannot believe he is asking me this question and I am tempted to dive back under. "You answer first."

"I've never kissed a girl," he says. "Not once."

"No way. Me neither."

"Very funny."

"Let's go under again."

I hold my breath and open my eyes underwater. Alex has bubbles under his nose and smiles at me tenderly.

We come back up and I can feel the electricity between us. Suddenly, I realize just how much he likes me and that it's way more complicated than I could ever conjure up in my imagination.

I think of Aurora Stone kissing Hoffman in the tree house and how maybe I don't need her anymore. Maybe I can have my own love story, which might not be perfect, but at least it's real.

"I'm sorry I ran away from you that day," he says. "It meant a lot what you said."

I am so preoccupied that I answer, "What did I say?"

"You know," he says, hesitating. "That you love me."

I feel embarrassed at hearing those words.

"It was so honest and truthful of you. I don't think anyone has ever spoken to me that way."

"Even though you don't feel the same?"

"Maybe I do. Maybe I don't. How are you supposed to know, anyway? I don't know anything about love."

"I don't know anything about it either," I say. "But it felt like you could read my mind and you made me feel like I am okay and could do anything."

He moves closer to me and I realize something is about to happen. Alex touches my shoulder and then his hands wrap around my back.

This time I close my eyes and wait.

Near the pool gate there's a sound. Someone is walking toward us. I open my eyes and see Josh Slater.

"Josh?" I ask in confusion. "What are you doing here?"

chapter twenty

"They flew us out for the show finale," Kat says, stepping forward from the shadows to meet with Josh. "Vivian thought it would make you feel better to have us here. She said you've been bummed out lately. I had this weird feeling you might be in the pool." Kat meets my eyes and stops abruptly. "Alyssa, is that you?"

"It's me," I say, realizing I'm not wearing my wig.

The camera crew is behind Kat and Josh, dragging their equipment and bright lights into the pool area.

"I thought we talked about no more surprises," I say under my breath.

I duck deep beneath the water, swimming toward the darker deep end where my wig is waiting. When I reach the end, I come up for air and gasp, out of breath. Then pull myself out of the water and throw the wig over my wet head. Alex steps out of the pool in the shallow end looking ready to bolt.

I should have known that Vivian would pull a stunt like this. Why would she think I wanted to be followed back here, let alone have my so-called friends invited?

"Josh? Kat? I wasn't prepared for you guys," I say, apologetically, walking toward them, wishing a towel would magically appear. The crew is behind us getting in on the action.

"I guess not," Kat says, with a strange look on her face. "The show wanted the full story on you. What is going on? Did they make you shave your head?"

"Well, Vivian is the star here," I say, ignoring her question. "Most of the show isn't about me."

"Alyssa," Josh says, "There is something different about you. What is it?"

It's the first time Josh has spoken to me in months, other than our random text messages and small talk. And here he is asking me the one question I do not want to answer. I stare at the ground, unable to speak.

"She has a boyfriend," Alex says, coming up behind me and putting his arm around me.

"Alex," I hiss.

"Well, you do," he says. "Maybe that's what's different."

I glance at him, dazzled. Then Vivian breaks through the crowd, halting the film crew. When I see her, I know I am in big trouble. She is trying not to show it, but you can see the anger in her icicle eyes. I have outdone her, for once, here in my wet dress, nearly kissing a boy in the pool with my hair all gone.

I want to take off the wig and throw it at her. I want to scream at her to leave me alone. I want to tell her I am running away with Alex and leaving the country.

But as usual, I freeze up with my mouth sealed shut

Vivian lowers her voice to a whisper. "This is being filmed, Lissy. Read the cue cards."

I look from Vivian to Kat to Josh and then to Alex.

He smiles and raises his eyebrows, as if daring me.

Then I pull off my wig and throw it at the camera. It lands right on the lens.

Everyone is stunned silent and then Josh reaches out for the wig. In perfect Josh fashion, he trips over a cord and his glasses fall off. Then he slips into Vivian. She grabs onto him to steady herself and the two of them fall straight into the pool together with a splash.

"I'm such a klutz," Josh says, dripping in the water with Vivian struggling next to him to gain her composure.

Alex glances at me and takes my hand. "Ready?" he says. "One… two… three," and we leap into the deep end together.

Then Frankie yells, "Everyone in the pool!" and he does a nice little shove of Kat and the production crew. The next thing I know the partygoers are all lining up and jumping into the pool and this dark, peaceful place has turned into chaos.

"These ratings are gonna fly through the roof," Mighty Mike chimes in, taking off his tuxedo jacket and doing a cannonball.

I tread water, doing a quick check to make sure Alex can make it to the shallow end. He grabs the side of the pool, looking nervous, but gives me a thumbs-up.

Since everyone is half drunk, there is splashing and wrestling and people laughing crazily like wild college kids. Everyone, that is, except for Vivian, who I suddenly realize looks very different herself.

Her hair, which had been styled at the top of her head, has fallen down like a stack of dominoes. She tries to stack it back in place, but the mass of hair is flattened.

I have to look twice before I realize something is wrong.

Very wrong.

"You shouldn't have come back here," Vivian says, watching me carefully and moving herself into the darkness. She is about the ugliest person in the pool right now, her hair and makeup destroyed.

I swim ahead, my eyes on her wet hair. It just doesn't look right. I cannot believe what is in front of me.

"That's not your real hair, is it?" I say, in shock. I am holding on to the edge in the deep end. I can't believe I never noticed before.

Suddenly I am floating above the pool and this party and the yard and earth above and right into the stars. It's kind of like my life flashing right before my eyes. I see Vivian and all of our conversations projected in front of me. My head is on her shoulder in the living room. I see her comforting me with lies.

"How could you?" I say, splashing water at her in anger. "I always thought we had nothing in common, that maybe I was switched at birth. Why didn't you just tell me the truth?"

"I was trying to protect you," she whispers, splashing back. "I thought if I told you, that it would make it worse. I thought that you would give up too soon."

"But you took me to that group," I say, with another defiant splash. "And you didn't say a word."

"I'm sorry," she whispers. "I have a career. It doesn't allow me to go public with this kind of thing." She raises her eyebrows, as if to say *end of story or I'll kill you.*

"I wouldn't tell anyone," I say, trying to hide my hurt. "But I don't think you would do the same for me."

Vivian is silent, as she hurries toward the ladder. She holds her acrylic nails up toward her mass of fake hair, glancing nervously around her.

"Don't you dare," she mouths at me. She looks so different in the water now, her hair and makeup undone, that I realize I didn't know just how much she was hiding. Vivian is my mother, but she is slowly slipping away. She has become someone else, someone I cannot recognize.

People are exiting the pool area, drying off with a stack of towels. Vivian throws one over her head and around her shoulders, lifting herself up the ladder in her sopping wet red Barbie dress.

Kat follows, glancing at me in confusion. Alex is talking to Frankie as they sit in a couple lawn chairs near the mermaid statue reviewing the film clips.

I want Vivian as far away as possible. I am afraid what might come out of my mouth if we are thrown together in a room. I feel our conversations about my hair creeping into my memory, sinking to my gut. It is all so disturbing that I don't even realize it when Josh is right in front of me.

"Hey," he says. "What a night, huh?"

"That's an understatement."

"You do look pretty awesome," he says, gesturing at my head. "I've always enjoyed staring at you."

I hesitate. "Thanks. I think."

I can smell a trace of alcohol on his breath and we paddle together toward the shallow end. "I don't know too many girls who can pull off that look," he continues. "Except you should try wearing a bikini next time you're in the pool."

"Right," I say, remembering my adoration for him all these years and how I don't care so much anymore.

I never imagined I'd be facing Josh without my curly hair enveloping over my shoulders.

"I think this move has been good for you," he adds.

I blush. "I think you're slightly crazy. Let's get out of the pool, okay?"

"You're calling me crazy?" Josh says. "You're the one who shaved your head."

"It really wasn't something I wanted to do. Can we please not talk about it?"

"Relax, okay? You should try some of the drinks they're making at the bar. Delish."

"I don't want anything, Josh."

"Is this why you moved? You know, your hair?"

I shake my head. "It's just something that happened, you know?"

Josh frowns. "Is it going to grow back?"

"Someday. I hope so."

"Are you okay otherwise?"

"I guess that depends on how you define okay."

I suddenly realize that maybe my hair won't grow back. Maybe I will always look this way and maybe I will still be okay. This is pretty much my worst fear right here and I am with Josh and he is gazing at me adoringly and the world isn't ending.

"Do you remember when we tried to kiss that one time?" he asks, smiling. "We were playing that game in Kat's basement."

"Yes," I say, surprised to hear him mention it. Then he takes my waist and lifts me up playfully.

I giggle, unable to help myself. "I'm surprised you remember it too," I say. "I got nervous and ran into the bathroom."

"I was disappointed," he says.

"Yeah, right," I say, unable to keep myself from smiling bigger. "I still can't believe you and Kat are here right now and no one told me you were coming. These people who run this show are evil, I tell you."

Except for Frankie.

"Your mom thought you would be excited to see us."

She is not my mom, I want to say. *I don't know who she is anymore.*

"Kat is just a friend," he adds. "Always has been."

"That's not what I hear. I know what happened."

"Well," he says, "I know who I wanted, but you moved away."

"Come on, Josh…"

He leans into me.

"You're way hotter than Kat. You know that, right? Don't forget that."

I can feel his breath hot on my face and I realize how much has changed. I push him back, my hand stopping him right in front of his chest. Josh looks at me, surprised.

"Let's get out of here," I say. "I need some dry clothes."

Frankie is at the back door, handing out courtesy sweat suits. Apparently one of the crew members had orders to run out and get enough clothing for all the drenched partygoers.

Frankie hands me a blue sweat suit set. "Where is your mother?" he asks. "Everyone is looking for her."

"I don't know," I say, as he adds a baseball cap to the pile of clothes.

"Would you please tell me if you see her?" he asks. "The crew is kind of worried. Mighty Mike is pacing around the house like a frantic zoo animal."

"I will," I say, wondering if she is even recognizable right now with her hair and makeup messed up. "I'm sure she'll turn up."

Honestly, I don't care where Vivian is and I hope she doesn't care where I am either. Soon we'll be driving back to San Diego together, pretending again that everything is okay and that none of this happened. I can see it now. She'll have a contract for me to sign that says I won't tell anyone *her* secret.

I search the hallways and elaborate rooms for Alex, and wander back outside to the back yard.

"Party's over, kids," Mighty Mike says, wearing a red bathrobe with sneakers and pacing near the back door with his phone to his ear. "Until next season."

Where are you? I text, nervous that Alex may be gone forever again.

"Alyssa," Kat says, finding me in the dimly lit hallway with all of the grandmother photos. She looks beautiful, as usual, even with her wet hair combed back and blue sweat suit that matches mine.

"I cannot believe what you did earlier," she says. "What happened to your hair?"

"Well, it's gone," I say, stating the obvious. "Look, I really had no idea you and Josh were coming tonight and I don't want you guys here." I push the baseball cap further down. "I'm in no place to have visitors. Vivian should have known. Plus, with everything that has happened…" My voice trails off.

"I thought you weren't mad," Kat says.

"I don't know what I feel anymore."

"It's all right," she says. "I get it. The show gave us a free trip. They wanted to send your dad out, but I guess Vivian axed the idea."

"Big surprise. She's always axing things."

"By the way, I practiced a new cheer I want to show you," she says, as if our friendship is still intact. She lowers her voice. "But I wasn't sure if you were too sick to jump around." She motions at my head. "I didn't realize you had cancer. Why didn't you tell me?"

"I don't have cancer," I explain, my stomach hollow. "And I don't want to practice any cheers right now."

"Well, we've got two rooms in our hotel. Do you want to come back and join us and we can talk? I think Josh wants to see you some more. You know I'm so over him."

"No. Go away, Kat."

Then I leave her alone, realizing how odd it feels to say no to Kat. It feels odd and good.

"Alyssa?" Kat says in protest. "I don't understand. What has happened to you, anyway?"

I'm standing on the sidewalk. Alex writes.

I'm already out the front door, walking quickly.

In front of the house? I ask.

The school bus stop. Remember where we got dropped off?

I'm sliding into the seat next to the golf cart driver taking people to their cars.

I think so.

Meet me?

I head down the driveway, sending Vivian a text: *Everyone is looking for you. Might want to come out of your hiding spot. Carpe diem.*

chapter twenty-one

The next morning I wake up in an unfamiliar bedroom with boxes packed all around me. They reach all the way to the ceiling and I suddenly wonder if I'm dreaming.

A ceiling fan is whirling above my head and I watch it spinning. There is a boy next to me asleep. *My boyfriend!* He is snoring lightly. *I am in his bedroom!* I still can't believe he called himself my boyfriend, which technically makes me his girlfriend. His arms are around me and have been that way all night. I close my eyes again, wishing hard that we could stay like this forever.

Even though nothing out of the ordinary has happened, not even a kiss, I am delighted. I slept next to Alex and that feels good and right. Last night his brother borrowed the car to pick us up and we got to his house, exhausted. And here we are now. Waking up together as the sun rises.

I am still in my blue sweat suit and my baseball cap is on the floor next to the mattress. I'll probably put it on when Alex opens his eyes, but for now I can simply listen to his breathing.

It calms my thoughts, which are starting to race.

I cannot remember what happened to my wig last night. I hope someone grabbed it. I hope Vivian doesn't kill me for disappearing. I guess we both made disappearances last night.

An airplane flies overhead.

"Alex?" I ask.

"Yeah," he says, stirring.

"Are you awake?"

"I am now." He turns to me, groggy.

"Good morning."

"Look at your eyes," he says. "They are deep blue like the ocean. I'll remember them this way. They are perfection."

I smile, feeling him slipping away, already up in the air and crossing the border and no longer next to me. I hesitate, and then I just say what I'm thinking because it really doesn't matter anymore. "Do you think you can kiss me before you go? Like, if I don't kiss you, I'm not sure if anyone will ever kiss me."

"Someone will kiss you," he says. "I know that for sure."

"Well, you're technically my boyfriend," I reply. "At least for the next few hours. And you're the last guy I really liked who knew me with all my hair. So, you have a memory of my brown curls and that I'm sometimes pretty."

"You're always pretty, Alyssa," he says. "I'm not sure how many different ways I can say it."

"I don't feel pretty. I'm scared of going back to my old school and leaving this place. It's easier to be brave here. I don't know how I'm going to face everyone and their questions."

"You can still wear a wig, right?"

"Oh yeah. Hopefully Vivian will buy me a better one this

time or maybe some kind of hair implants. I'm not going to school without one."

"So maybe people won't even find out."

"Alex, I think we were on TV last night and it's probably all over the Internet by now. Plus, I know the most popular girl in my class—my so-called best friend—won't keep her mouth shut. She has never been good at that."

"Then, I say let other people say and do what they want. They aren't you."

"She thinks I have cancer. I don't have cancer, Alex."

I look down, ready to cry.

"Come here," he says, holding me closer. I feel his heart beat against mine and my thoughts slow down again.

Then Alex sits up and grabs a notebook. He jots something down on the bottom of a bunch of a lines and then rips out a page, putting it in an envelope.

"I know you can get better. This is for you," he says. "For you to read later." He stands up and stretches his arms. "I do need to finish packing and get ready to go to the airport. I don't want to, but I have to keep getting ready."

What about that kiss?

I realize I'm not sure what I should do or where I should go next. To Vivian's hotel? To Rachel's? To Kat and Josh's hotel?

"I wish I could just come with you," I add.

"Me too," he says. "But it's impossible. Plus, I'll be back some day and I need someone to visit in our home town."

"When did you say you'll move back?"

"Maybe a couple months or a couple years, but who knows? It'll be some day. That's for sure."

Some day, I repeat in my head.

Alex leaves the room and comes back wearing a pair of shorts and a t-shirt with his red sneakers. I notice the shark tooth necklace and his dark, mysterious eyes and I'm crazy nervous just like the first time we met.

He takes my hand, helping me up. "Marcos says he can drive you home now. You should go before it gets any later."

"Okay," I say, focusing around the room to look for my stuff, and then I realize I don't have anything with me other than my baseball cap and the envelope Alex just gave me.

"Did you forget anything?" he asks.

"I feel like I did, but this is all I brought with me."

I feel silly all of a sudden in this oversized sweat suit and baseball cap and knowing this is how Alex is going to remember me. At least I don't have to worry about my hair being messed up first thing in the morning.

"Oh wait, I know what you forgot," he says suddenly.

"What?" I ask, confused and glancing around again.

The morning sunlight is lined up just right through the window, just like I've imagined before. Alex comes closer to me, cupping my face in his hands and I close my eyes.

This time he kisses me for real.

It's a goodbye kiss, but it's perfect.

#1 Alex.

chapter twenty-two

These are the contents of the folded-up letter that I open up later:

These are the things I want you to remember:
Some day I hope to see you again.
I don't think I'll be gone more than three years.
I think you could grow your hair back by then.
Or maybe not. But you should try.
Maybe you'll fail, maybe not. I'm with you either way.
That's 1,095 days.
It all starts with one day and goes from there.
One day.
That's how we'll count the time between now and then.
Day by day.
Hair by hair.
I love you.

acknowledgments

Thanks to anyone and everyone who listened to me talk about this book and my journey with it. Thanks to my entire family for their support, and especially my parents. A special thanks to Amy Johnson who helped me edit a previous version, and thanks to Wendy Crook who gave me a beautiful cover design and logo. Thanks to Jan Hamer for helping me polish up the final draft, and thanks to Alison McLennan for her timely advice. Thanks to Christina Pearson from the Trichotillomania Learning Center who read an earlier version and gave me her stamp of approval. And thanks to Leigh and Lindsey Cohn for being great employers when I was first working on this project.

I've been writing this book for so long I'm sure I've forgotten people to thank, but just know, your support and kindness has been appreciated. I'm glad I didn't give up on this.

about the author

Lindsay Woolman has always had a burning desire to write books. She grew up in Ogden, UT, and has lived all over the West, including Boise, ID, and Portland, OR. She currently lives and writes in San Diego, CA. *The Perfect Pull* is her first novel.

37728624R00115

Made in the USA
San Bernardino, CA
24 August 2016